I0539182

Table Of Contents

DIVE IN

Blockheads Workshop was established in 2019 when three lifelong friends found themselves sharing their daydreams and developing them into written stories. As Blockheads, we don't just put pen to paper with the desire to create something readable—we create ethereal experiences that transform a room into a ship in the center of a foreign and frosty sea or a couch into a cramped seat on a train, steaming toward a dark mountain tunnel.

Each book and short story contains an untouched world that's been written to life, every page ready to immerse you in something you've never experienced until this very moment. So, what are you waiting for? Stretch the book wide until the spine crinkles, breathe deep, and dive in.

★★★★★

www.blockheadsworkshop.com

Dedicated to C.M.C.

Text © 2025 Christian Mallia
Illustrations © 2025 Christian Mallia
Contributions by: Cole Nasta, Sean Nasta

ISBN: 978-1-7340743-0-7 (Ebook)
ISBN: 978-1-7340743-2-1 (Paperback)
Library Of Congress Control Number: 2025911892

All rights reserved. This book, or any portion thereof, may not be reproduced or used in any manner without the express written permission of the publisher, except for brief quotations in a book review. This is a work of fiction. Names, characters, businesses, places, events, and incidents are products of the author's imagination and are used fictitiously. Any resemblance to actual persons, living or dead, or actual events is purely coincidental.

To contact the author, please reach out at
hello@blockheadsworkshop.com

PART I:
ORDINARY WORLD

Not long ago, the spirit of the land, known as Freyacre, was alive and vibrant. Before man's fire and axe severed its limbs, and the horse and plow ravaged its heart, the spirit delighted in observing the intricate web of life it sustained. With a steadfast gaze unlike any of its creatures, it watched from the soil and roots, grass, rocks, moss, and riverbeds, and every precipice, whether tree or cliff. Yet, despite its many eyes, each creature only ever caught fleeting glimpses of the spirit.

The eagle scanned the canyons from a nest high in the spirit's crown, where the mountaintops kissed the sky, while the rabbit burrowed deep into its womb, where every mighty tree and fruitful shrub had once been birthed. The fish swam through its veins, unless blocked by a beaver's dam, while the bear stared into those veins, waiting to catch a fish. The squirrel clung to one of the spirit's fingers, peeking upside down at the world below, while the snake slithered unseen through the thicket of the spirit's skin, oblivious to the squirrel above.

All creatures thrived on the spirit's generous bounty, whether they realized it or not, and were even gifted the ability to understand one another through a language not of words, but purrs, chirps, squeaks, chatter, thumps, bugles, hisses, growls, and snarls.

Though the spirit played no favorites, for that would go against its nature, it did keep a closer watch on some. And it was there to witness the birth of the elk calf, White Snout, nestled against the spirit's chest in a golden wheat field.

She grew up amidst a large and peaceful herd, sheltered from danger. Her father, Red Thorn, ranked fifth among the twelve bull leaders and strode proudly at the center of the herd, surrounded by his harem of many cows and offspring, too preoccupied to give anyone his full attention for long.

From her mother, Long Neck, she inherited the unspoken wisdom of the forest; how to thread through trails, dart between trees while avoiding thorns, and hide by pressing her body against the earth. Her mother showed her where to find the tenderest shoots and scolded her for sniffing at plants that would poison. Together, they would prick their ears to listen for the babbling of a nearby stream, taking turns drinking, so one could always watch their surroundings. Yet, the importance of these lessons would soon slip from White Snout's mind whenever she rejoined her half-siblings and the other calves of the herd.

They spent their days playing endless games. One was River Cross, where the challenge was to stay dry to win. Another was Lock, Dodge, or Leap, a test of strength dominated by the young bulls. White Snout's favorite, though, was Chase-and-Hide, because she knew the best twists in the trails when being pursued and retreated to the most secret spots when she wasn't.

Rounds often ended with her name bugled in surrender, and she tried her best not to seem too smitten by victory as she strutted out from cover. To her, this was the pure joy of calfhood, and she sometimes resented being pulled away by her mother for lessons the other mothers dismissed as archaic. But still, Long Neck insisted that danger was always lurking.

As White Snout lay curled beside her mother at night, she would gaze up at the countless twinkling stars, letting her imagination drift with the forest's whispers. When Long Neck rose, careful not to disturb her, White Snout pretended to sleep, but secretly watched as her mother approached Red Thorn, who sprawled among the other cows in his harem. *Blight*, *storm*, and *fire* were the names of nightmares her mother warned about, but one danger was more terrifying than all the others, the very name a curse to be shunned—*wolf*.

"I have never seen such a beast, nor did my father's father," Red Thorn would say, unperturbed.

Sometimes, another cow would add to the ridicule. "Can you not enjoy the peace the leaders have won for us?"

But even in the face of rejection, Long Neck would stand firm, stomping her hoof in defiance. "The seasons turn no matter how much we love the summer. We have safety now, but this too will pass."

However, the further Long Neck echoed her concerns, the more she was rejected and ultimately dismissed. And while these faceless terrors made White Snout tremble, even her fears would soon yield to the splendor of dreams upon her mother's return and her soothing caress.

As one dream faded into the next, so too did the seasons of White Snout's calfhood. Limbs lengthened, and white spots on her coat were chased away by brown fur. The only remnant of her youthful colorings was her snout, still as milky white as ever. Though she danced through the forest with the graceful form of a maturing cow, her spirit remained that of a calf; nurtured, naive, and protected from danger under her mother's ever-vigilant watch.

A year passed in this idyllic fashion. Yet, as she continued to play whenever she could escape her mother's lessons, her thoughts began to stray further from games and drift toward curiosity—and the truth behind her mother's warnings. Curiosity, however, is the death of innocence, and it burned hot within her. By the time her second summer arrived, she had started eavesdropping more on the elders' gossip, and it was during this reckless frolic that she accidentally discovered love.

His name was Sharp, bestowed upon him for the antler knobs he had since birth, a rarity none had seen before. When they were younger, White Snout loved to play with him. But now, as he approached his third summer, he had grown rough and was the fastest of his peers. His once-small knobs had blossomed into a magnificent young crown.

Naturally, as the male calves came bucking into bullhood, they became aggressive in their play, pursuing the female offspring until one of the twelve leaders took notice and chased them away into the wilderness to start a harem of their own. Though Sharp had a different approach.

Instead of vying for the attention of the females as expected, he became a patient student, delving into the intricacies of the forest and inquiring about the traditions the herd upheld. His keen interest and respectful demeanor were welcomed by the elders, both bull and cow alike, and they enjoyed the pleasant conversations his questions would spark. This allowed White Snout to learn vicariously from afar much of the wisdom the elks had to offer—all except for Broadhoof, that is.

"How did the number of leaders in a herd come to be twelve? Why not thirteen, or thirty?" Sharp inquired of the elder bulls one day while they grazed in a field.

"Ha!" snorted Broadhoof in derision. "Why not plunge into thornbushes instead of traveling well-worn paths? You threaten the herd with these digging questions. Begone, and let the forest teach you!"

Broadhoof held the lowest rank among the twelve, a position he'd fallen to over the years. To him, the youngling's questions were meddlesome. While others praised, he mocked, finding joy in tormenting Sharp.

"Let him ask. A path blindly followed leads to doom. We should share the wisdom of what lies ahead," said Great Horn, the highest ranking and eldest of the herd. While this might seem kind of him, underneath a shallow, stoic façade, he was truly a glutton for drama, drooling at the chance to pit two bulls against each other.

Broadhoof stomped the ground and shook his head. "He should have been cast out long ago. And it's my right to chase him into the prickers." He stared at Great Horn, who made the slightest hum of amusement.

After a long pause, the great elk nodded. "It *is* your right as a ranking leader. The decision is yours."

It was apparent in Broadhoof's stride how ecstatic he was with Great Horn's approval as he rushed over to kick Sharp in the flank to seal his exile. But as he lifted a hoof and delivered it backward, his attack met only air. Sharp had already dashed clear away and stood with his hooves planted and his antlers lowered. He stomped the earth three times, the formal signal of a duel.

"By the traditions of our elders, you cast me out. By that same tradition, I challenge you for your rank."

Broadhoof gaped dumbly at him, though his eyes betrayed a flicker of concern. "Dueling is reserved for the Rut."

"Not necessarily," Great Horn interjected, excitement plainly etched across his face. "It's unconventional... and conceivably unwise, but no tradition has been violated."

The other bulls were listening between mouthfuls of dandelions and clovers, but as the tension built, they gradually came to encircle them. Broadhoof glanced about his brethren but found no friends, only spectators eager for sport.

Cornered, Broadhoof stomped the ground thrice with a strength that Sharp lacked. He was bigger than Sharp, a seasoned grown bull, nearly twice as wide with double the number of points on his antlers—a seemingly guaranteed victory. Letting out a thundering bugle, the anthem of battle, Broadhoof exploded into a charge with a speed that defied his age.

But the young buck escaped the sweep of his opponent's antlers with practiced movement, redirecting the charge with a low angled dodge to the left and a well-timed twist of his neck to the right. Sharp's antler pricked the flank of the elder bull's rear leg, instantly drawing blood. Broadhoof bellowed again, but this time not in rage, but in pain.

Before Broadhoof could properly wheel around, Sharp moved as swiftly and as effortlessly as the wind, leaping eye-level with his opponent and plowing a bloody furrow with a spike across Broadhoof's forehead. But even wounded, the old buck rose on his back hooves and brought down the front with all his weight. Sharp's agility could not save him from the blow.

White Snout was some distance off when she heard the commotion and saw the other cows and calves rushing to the source. Slipping under the bellies of several taller cows, she peered through the forest of legs. In the center of it all, Broadhoof threw his antlers in every direction and bucked his rear legs into the air. There was a gory mark on his forehead, blood streaming down into his eyes.

Great Horn delighted in the carnage. "Blinded by blood! Well fought, young Sharp. Now let's see if you can finish it."

But Sharp made no attempt to strike his wounded foe. Instead, he kept just out of reach, dodging ill-aimed attacks that drained Broadhoof's stamina. He remembered the battering of hooves and would not risk suffering them again.

Recognizing Sharp's strategy, Great Horn switched from encouraging him to deliver a grand finish to heckling Broadhoof. "Can't put down a third year, aye? You've spent too much time in the berry bushes and chasing cows."

Broadhoof, however, did not hear the jibe or notice that the whole herd had gathered, that his harem watched in fear and his brethren in anticipation. The old elk twisted his neck, swinging wildly at the air. His attacks were impotent, merely the last shred of his honor dying along with his breath. Finally, he stood in the center of his herd, wheezing, bleeding, and broken.

There was no need to cast out the withering elk. He merely limped forward, his former brethren parting on either side and making a path for him to leave. Before he made his final retreat, Great Horn laughed and said to Sharp, "deliver a kick and send him to exile!"

Sharp's leg twitched, about to take a step forward at his hierarch's command, but he couldn't. Under other circumstances, Great Horn might remind Sharp of his authority, but for now, he catered to the audience. "Embarrassment shall be punishment enough!"

After the defeated bull disappeared into the distance, Great Horn declared Sharp as the victor and noted that Broadhoof's harem would be redistributed at the next Rut, unless they felt the desire to follow him into the wilderness. None did. It was an odd christening for a new leader, where the herd welcomed the permanence of Sharp but mourned the loss of Broadhoof.

As Sharp bowed before each of his—well, now—fellow brethren, starting with the eleventh and ending before Great Horn, who nodded in return, White Snout was overcome by a new feeling deep in the pit of her stomach, as if she had swallowed a hot stone.

Violence, not the playful roughhousing she was accustomed to, had broken into her world. The elders seemed as everlasting as the mountains or the sky, but this had shaken the very bedrock of her understanding. Her mind struggled to wrap around this abrupt reality, one no longer centered on play but rooted in the harsh truths of their nature.

As her thoughts raced, Sharp turned to look out at the entire herd, his fur ruffled and standing on end, but his hide otherwise unharmed. He appeared no different than after an afternoon of rowdy play, except his normally golden-velvet antlers now glistened scarlet, their tips dripping with Broadhoof's blood. For a moment, White Snout caught Sharp's gaze, and he nodded, making her tail flutter.

Great Horn, though the most powerful, was still very old, and his wrinkles deepened with exhaustion. With the excitement over, he wandered off with three of his cows to a nearby spot where the grass gave way to flat stone, heated by the high sun, offering a pleasant place for a nap. The rest of the herd resumed their usual activities as if the fight had never happened.

Then there was Sharp, who, despite his victory, was a leader without followers. He trotted in the opposite direction of Great Horn, descending a shallow slope that soon disappeared from view, but White Snout knew there was a small lake beyond. Curious, she followed.

She hid behind a tree as Sharp approached the water's edge, dipping an antler into the shallows and stirring the water red before it quickly cleared again. He lifted his head and stood as still as the trees, waiting until the final droplets fell from his antlers and the ripples in the water faded. His gaze slowly swept across the vast landscape before him, its end never in sight.

"The leaves are turning. Autumn's coming," he said simply.

The same feeling of swallowing a hot stone crept into White Snout's stomach. They were calfhood friends and had spent countless passing suns chasing after one another. She had spent just as many shadowing him as he pursued greater knowledge, though a moment like this was undiscovered. She was at a loss for what to say.

He turned his head, and their eyes met as she revealed herself from behind the tree. She came closer to him until her hooves were also in the water. A minnow danced between them.

"You know, I don't know what came over me either," he said, his gaze returning to the landscape. They were only a year apart, but he felt older to her. "What happened doesn't feel real, as if the part of myself that challenged Broadhoof was a part of me I'm still getting to know... a scarier side. I've played with his offspring. Now, I'll forever be the elk that displaced his family." His head dropped.

At this, her heart ached. The thought hadn't crossed her mind, yet it already weighed so heavily on his. She lowered her head and nudged his chin upright.

"No, you stood up for yourself," she said with conviction. As he was forced into a new role, she became his support. "They will say you were brave, and that he lost his way."

"Will they?" he said despondently.

"Of course they will. You deserve to be up there, Sharp. Never has a third year challenged an elder, much less won. You proved yourself worthy in front of our whole herd, and I for one am proud to call you my leader."

"Well, becoming a leader—"

"No, a rightful leader already," she affirmed. "You've been practicing far before today. Just who could've guessed how it played out, huh?"

"I sure didn't," he said, a small hum escaping him. He butted her neck gently with his forehead. "Thanks for coming here with me. I'm sure you already know this, but I take comfort in your company."

She had always wondered if she annoyed Sharp in her quest for knowledge and subsequent eavesdropping. It eased her to know he felt otherwise.

"Even though we're getting older," he continued. "You remind me of a simpler time when I didn't have a care in the world. Remember when we teamed up and rammed into Stoneback's side so hard, we tipped him over?"

She spun in amusement. "How could I forget? As soon as he caught on and chased us, he tripped over his own hooves and fell again!"

Sharp matched her joy with a hearty chuckle. "He was so angry!"

For a moment, she felt his heart leap in innocent joy, but then a slight chill blew, and he immediately masked the lightheartedness with a stern face. He was becoming a leader.

"Are you scared?" she asked, knowing what he was feeling in a way only good friends could.

He hesitated to admit what was blatantly on his face. "A little. We had such a peaceful calfhood, but now, I'm not able to play games anymore."

White Snout recognized that while they were similar in age, he likely still viewed her as a calf. Just this morning, she rolled in the grassy fields and reveled in the softness, while he was already noticing the leaves turning brown and planning ahead. She wished she could lighten his burden, to share in the responsibility that had been bestowed upon him. But being young and female, this wasn't her role. Perhaps, what little she could offer would soothe his knitted brow.

She tilted her head to gaze up at him and spoke with love and intent in the hopes that even if her message meant little, the admiration with which she conveyed it would rekindle his spirit. "Sharp, you're the strongest elk I know. If anyone is ready to help lead us, it's you."

Her gesture was a success, and he hid his joy by dipping his head to take another drink of water. She couldn't believe this was the same bull whose legs wobbled not long ago.

"Thank you. You're a real friend who's always been there for me."

Like asking if he was scared, the next line spilled out of her from the same secret haven within her heart only good friends shared. "And I always will."

They both released a restrained breath as a piney gust slipped between them, licking the lake's moisture off their ankles. They came closer, until Sharp playfully, yet tenderly, bumped his nose against hers.

"I've never told you how beautiful you are. Where on earth did that white snout come from anyway?"

She curled her neck so that her chin met her shoulder. The elder bulls often complimented her throughout her calfhood on how unique her beauty was, but never had he; it sounded best from him.

"My mother always said it's a gift from Freyacre."

He nodded, and a perfect moment transpired. Then, his stare shifted past her, pupils growing wide. "Speaking of, she's coming. I hope you'll forgive me for this."

Before White Snout understood his meaning, he stomped the shallow water, splashing it up into her face. Instead of becoming annoyed, she peered at him from behind the droplets that spilled through her fur, his uncertainty about his action making him resemble a calf anticipating he was in trouble. Her heart swelled with warmth.

"Oh no you didn't," she said, lowering her head and stomping the ground thrice, mimicking the acceptance for a duel. She charged and bumped playfully into his side in an attempt to reenact how they tipped over Stoneback, though she was unsuccessful in knocking over Sharp. And in that moment, as Long Neck shook her head before retreating to join the company of her fellow cows, White Snout and Sharp's once quiet conversation evolved into a playful wrestle where, for a time, they were innocent calves again.

PART II:
WOLF ORDEAL

L ike Sharp had observed, the once lush greens of summer quickly faded with each passing day. Freyacre was preparing for hibernation, stretching across the land and coaxing the trees to shed their leaves in brilliant displays of fiery red, burnt orange, and golden yellow, signaling to all creatures that autumn was upon them.

In response to the spirit's call, the bulls grew new, larger antlers. Their fur thickened and scents became more pungent. Aggression simmered just beneath the surface, evident in their stiff postures, clenched teeth, and snorts during casual exchanges, each encounter laced with thinly veiled hostility. The air around them buzzed with tension, revealing a certain readiness for what was to come. Though the time to duel had not yet arrived, it loomed ever closer, the spirit reminding them with each breath of cold air replacing the warmth that once lingered that nature's grand contest was fast approaching.

White Snout was in her second year and knew what was upon them—the famed "Rut" so many gossiped about. Although her mother had kept her at a distance during her first year, she remembered traveling to a secluded place where the valley walls touched the sky. She recalled the sounds as she pressed her ears against her mother's stomach, a repetitive, piercing noise, like a mighty oak snapping at its trunk. However, this year was different. She was more mature and regarded by her herd as a cow instead of a calf. But even though her mother had explained what the Rut was, she still didn't quite grasp what the Rut *actually* was and wouldn't embarrass herself by admitting otherwise.

"The twelve leaders will pick from the second-year cows, and then you will belong to them, as I belong to your father," Long Neck instructed her daughter. White Snout nodded, pretending to comprehend, pretending to have courage, but her mother knew better. "Don't you worry, little one. At the end, we'll still be in the same herd, just different harems."

With her mother's assurance, White Snout was ready to face the unknown. Her body felt different, strange yet eager, yearning to participate in this Rut without knowing why. More importantly, she wanted to be there to support Sharp.

When the first leaves fell from their trees and the time for the Rut was upon them, she, along with the dozens of other second-year cows and their mothers, was led by the twelve bull leaders a day's journey away to an intimate field at the bottom of a valley. The walls, as White Snout's memory recalled correctly, surrounded them on all sides except the narrow inlet they entered through, blocking the horizon from view while the sun hung directly overhead.

She wanted to be brave, but by the way the elder bulls goggled at her with wet noses and loose jaws as she trotted by (except for Sharp and her father, Red Thorn), she wished to retreat to her mother's side. What was happening, despite her best efforts to act ready, ultimately remained a mystery to her—a mystery she wasn't yet fully aware she'd be happy to unveil.

Once every cow had gathered in the valley, Great Horn walked slowly to the edge of the field where the ground surrendered to the slope. Coming into position, he stomped the earth with a mighty front hoof, causing the nearby birds to flee from their nests and a shiver to shoot up White Snout's spine. Though the eldest of the herd, the leader of leaders intimidated every elk by his sheer size, for even the second largest of the herd disappeared when standing behind him. He allowed a harrowing silence to dominate the air as he swayed his neck sluggishly from side to side, his eyes feasting on the new prospects.

"Separate," he commanded. His voice was low and deep, and although he didn't speak loudly, it carried, bouncing off the valley walls so that nothing was unheard.

Long Neck turned to her daughter, her expression marked by grave seriousness. It struck White Snout in her knees, causing them to wobble like a calf's. "My daughter, on this day you become a cow. Be strong, and I will rejoin you at the end."

White Snout remained trembling in place as her mother and the other cows assembled in a group behind them. The twelve bulls formed a line according to rank in front, leaving all the second years idling in the middle of the field at the bottom of the walled-in valley.

With the younglings left unaccompanied before Great Horn, a sudden wetness gleamed on his cracked lips, the saliva drying into a white paste where the corners met. As he crept closer to them, his musk wafted forward, making White Snout gag even from where she stood in the middle of the crowd.

"Welcome, all of you, to the Rut. For those bulls who have been here before, you know how this goes, and for the one who has not—" Great Horn nodded at Sharp. "You'll quickly learn. This is your chance to prove yourselves and make any cow you desire your own. As per the traditions of our fathers, and their fathers before them, the leaders will select accordingly from left to right, or highest-ranking member to lowest-ranking member, from the available cows until they all belong.

Cows, when selected, you'll come forward, bow before your new mate, and stand behind him. Bulls, if you wish to challenge your position in line, feel free to do so, but I caution you... it could cost you your life."

He paused, allowing the silence to emphasize the severity of his message.

"I invite you all to share a vision with me. Beauty... true beauty... cannot be described. Some have tried. Some have captured a fleeting glimpse in song, but the odd thing about beauty is... it's always slipping away. It's something we will eternally covet. We gaze upon and miss it before it's gone. We dedicate rituals to it. It's in our nature to sacrifice our very lives in order to protect it. But for each that possesses beauty... there is a threat seeking to steal it. My father once said, 'son, when you become leader, you'll have the power to pick from all the beauty of the world as you see fit… but it'll come at a cost'. You see, he understood, even then, that—"

Great Horn's speech dragged on, his words stretching into what felt like an eternity. He abandoned his position, pacing sluggishly back and forth, pausing at random to gaze up at the sky, as though his speech was etched in the clouds. He mentioned how their ancestors were watching them with pride whenever the stars appeared and that, on their final day, the spirit of Freyacre would welcome them home to a new earth if they upheld tradition. But White Snout heard none of it. Her ears were filled with the sound of her own heavy breathing as the true meaning of the Rut finally began to sink in.

She looked to Sharp, wondering if anyone had told him what was expected of him, or if he, like her, was now just realizing it. Except his face was as unreadable as stone, his attention fixed on Great Horn, aware of the countless eyes observing him. Whether he knew or not, they were both too far in to turn back now. Everyone they had ever known was watching.

The speech might have continued even longer, but Great Horn's eldest cow, sensing the herd's restlessness, gently huffed, giving him the nudge he needed to move forward. With that subtle prompt, Great Horn concluded his grand address, and the bulls began to growl, a low gurgling sound that spanned a few seconds before rising into a high-pitched scream, snapping White Snout out of her daze.

Though Sharp had always impressed her with his agility, strength, and wit, he seemed small and fragile standing at the end of the line compared to the other bulls beside him. It was foolish to think he could challenge even the eleventh strongest elk for a higher rank. All White Snout could do was hope she'd go unnoticed until it was Sharp's turn, so she could stand by his side for the rest of her life.

She looked over the backs of the other second-year cows surrounding her—friends, cousins, and half-siblings she'd grown close to in their youth, all with the same timidness as she—and made the difficult decision that it'd be better if they were picked over her. The odds were in her favor if she could remain hidden until Sharp's turn, and so she lowered her head to blend in with the crowd.

Starting at the left, Great Horn picked first, and no other bull dared to question it. Legend had it among the calves that he had killed the last elk to challenge his authority with one stomp, which was likely true given the way his brethren revered him. When he spoke, White Snout closed her eyes as his raspy voice pricked at her ears, almost too afraid to peek in case she was the one he so callously summoned. "You there, come to me."

Silence dominated the air again, and when White Snout eventually opened her eyes, she was relieved to see Petal, another young and sprightly second year, walk bashfully forward. Great Horn's sagging cheeks momentarily lifted as he watched his prize meet him with a bow and touch his forehead with her snout before coming to take her place behind him. All the while, Petal appeared miserable. When he turned back, he nodded to the bull beside him.

"Next," he said.

And just like that, the ritual of the Rut commenced. The third-placed bull challenged the second much to the delight of Great Horn, and a battle commenced, where the piercing snaps from White Snout's calfhood paid her a revisit, but this time even louder. She didn't want to watch, but twisted fascination gripped her, and she peeked up occasionally to see the opponents' antlers locked in a battle for dominance. Their shoulders were primed, their teeth grit, and their necks bulged with muscles as they shook their head intensely from side to side, attempting to catch the other in the ribs with an antler. It was beastly, violent, and everything White Snout couldn't bear to watch, and yet she did, forced to participate in the ferocious ritual set before her induction.

As she stood there, she felt like a first year again, petrified and in disbelief at how cruel bulls could be to one another when they were supposed to be brethren and bear the weight of leadership together. Whenever she was overwhelmed and nervousness got the better of her, she would glance at Sharp in the hope of gaining his attention. But she failed to do so, as he was too distracted by the show. So, she would look back at her mother, who was vigilantly watching her and able to soothe her regardless of distance.

A few rounds went by like this, where a bull would challenge the next higher up for their authority in line. Number three ascended to two. The new number three defended himself against four. Five, her father Red Thorn, stayed, while nine swapped spots with seven after winning back-to-back fights. Once each duel concluded, the victor would strut forward, scan the crowd of second years, select one, and return to his spot in line until his turn was upon him again. With every bull's announcement, White Snout's stomach flipped at the thought of being summoned with a callous, "you there, come to me." But to her fortune, after every call, she'd glance up to feel the same rush of relief when she discovered that another second-year cow was picked over her, and she was safe.

Eventually, ten picked without number eleven challenging him. When the eleventh-ranked elk passed over White Snout, Sharp remained silent, just as she had expected. He had barely secured his place among them, and it was clear he was content to avoid any fight. White Snout was certain he wouldn't make a move unless she was chosen by someone else. When his turn finally came, she quickly lifted her head from where she had been hiding, rising to her full height. At last, their eyes met, and the intensity of his gaze sent her heart fluttering.

Great Horn addressed the crowd, as he did at the beginning and end of each pick. "Alas, young Sharp, it's your turn, and no one will challenge your spot, for you are the last among us. Tell us then, which special cow before you will you honor as your very first."

Sharp strutted forward from the line with his head held high and his chest puffed. His antlers, just two points protruding from his skull, glistened gold in the sunlight that trickled over the valley walls. Though not much taller than the second-year cows, he was wider and more muscular, and despite lacking the size of the elder bulls, he was taut and fresh. White Snout swooned in his dark eyes as she bit her tongue in anticipation. Her plan was a success; she had saved herself for him, and her worries were now over. She could finally enjoy a moment of respite.

"Thank you, mighty Great Horn," Sharp said with an ostentatious bow, much to the old bull's pleasure. He, like the bulls before him, approached the crowd of second-year cows, and looking toward White Snout, who was no further than a pebble's toss away, said, "come to me, Round Eyes, for I have chosen you."

White Snout instinctively raised her hoof before it petrified in motion midair. Could he have just uttered what she so clearly heard? Could he have called another's name when her heart was unequivocally his, sealed in their moment by the lake… and perhaps before then too? He had called her beautiful. He had shared the same countless cheerful, wonderful, joyous moments with her throughout their calfhood. He was her love. Was she not his too? Weren't those beautiful, breathless moments equally cherished by him? Or was she simply a joke to him—someone he entertained momentarily before going off and coquetting with others?

Her heartbeat pulsed in her ears as the dreadful realization settled in. Another second year bounded forward from behind her, brushing her side. She couldn't fathom witnessing another live her dream, someone other than her rubbing their snout against Sharp's. The desire to flee to her mother's side or escape in any direction surged through her. What had she done to deserve this? She had only ever been kind to him, and he had shattered her trust in a single, swift action. She loved him. She thought he loved her. The pain in her chest felt as if it had been ripped open to bleed upon the earth, leaving her raw and exposed. In her anguish, she glanced back at her mother, who stood silent and still with a knowing gaze, sensing the betrayal.

But time can be cruel, and it didn't wait for White Snout to recover. It was already Great Horn's second-round pick. Once more, he slowly approached the cowering younglings, licking his lips and swiping away the lingering white paste with his tongue. The scene unfolded in front of her, yet White Snout remained trapped in the wreckage of her emotions.

"So many beauties," he cooed before swallowing hard. His musk filled White Snout's nostrils, dragging her back into the harsh reality she desperately sought to run away from. She shuddered when she came to, realizing her head was no longer lowered in hiding, but at its full height, unintentionally meeting her reflection in Great Horn's intense stare. His lips moved, ready to announce his decision.

But when he opened his mouth, another voice sounded. It too was low and deep, akin to Great Horn's, yet not marked by age. It resembled a growl emanating from a cave, echoing both near and far.

"So many beauties indeed," the voice said.

A creature loped through the single inlet of the valley. He was much smaller than Great Horn, perhaps a third in size, but his presence alone was enough to make the young cows huddle together in fear. He was unlike anything White Snout had ever seen; gray and magnificent, moving lithe and low with amber eyes, both focused and cruel. His snout was longer and sharper than an elk's, with two jagged teeth protruding from either side of his jaw. And his large paws, rivaling the size of a fox's, made no noise as they touched the ground. He kept his distance, circling the perimeter where the slope surrendered to the field, before leaping onto a boulder with the ease of a squirrel climbing a tree.

"Carnos," Great Horn said. "It's careless, even for you, to make yourself known during this day. What brings you to our esteemed Rut, when we are at our strongest?"

Carnos howled in amusement. "Do not deceive me. I've seen better days from you, once great one."

Perhaps no one else noticed, but White Snout caught sight of Great Horn's back leg buckling, his usual arrogance faltering. He was nervous, that much was clear, which he compensated for by speaking louder, which only made him appear weaker.

"If you're here to say something, then say it, but don't hold back our ceremonies with empty threats. Or be on your way!"

Carnos remained unflinching on his perch atop the boulder. His attention lingered on Great Horn before gazing out over the crowd with the same hungry expression the bulls did when the second years entered the heart of the valley.

"I always appreciated your bluntness, even if rude," Carnos remarked.

"OH, on with it!" Great Horn retorted, already tired of the gab.

"Very well." Carnos stepped down from the boulder. "I came to ask a trade from you. I represent many stomachs, a plight I'm sure you understand well. The other wolves of my pack are hungry, and I, as their leader, must provide."

Wolves? White Snout's thoughts spiraled, her mind flooding with a thousand nightmares. The snap of a twig, a rustle in the night—those sounds had always triggered her instinct to flee, but she had never been taught exactly what she was fleeing from. Her real-life experiences had been nothing more than a chipmunk dashing across a path or a vole scurrying through the underbrush. Over time, her brain had learned to downplay the fear, dismissing it as harmless creatures of the forest. But now, seeing this wolf before them, the mask that had once veiled her nightmares had been ripped away, and what stood before her was more terrifying than anything her imagination could have ever conjured. She finally understood her mother's lessons, the same lessons others had mocked for being overly cautious, even paranoid. Now, her warnings rang true with terrifying clarity.

"A trade, you say? Why would I trade with the likes of you?" Great Horn spat.

"Don't be cocky," Carnos growled. "I didn't come out in the open without proper precaution. There are many ready to strike should I signal. Tread with caution."

At this, Great Horn forgot to conceal his fear, quickly scanning the valley, but no creature could be seen.

Carnos continued. "We've been watching, waiting until you and the rest of you exhaust yourselves with your... games. We could've waited longer, until the veil of night was upon you, until you had mated so much you couldn't even stand properly, but we are more honorable than that. I do not wish to destroy a perfectly good herd, which is why I come to offer an exchange to honor the fathers before our time. An agreement was reached then, and we can do the same now."

He bared his teeth, perhaps attempting to show good faith, but instead caused a low gasp among the second years.

Great Horn seemed at a loss, and his voice trembled. "Well, what is it you propose?"

Carnos became bolder, stepping down from his perch and parading forward, so that he and Great Horn's chest were just a branch apart. Standing now, White Snout spotted a long, gray tail that dusted the earth behind him like a fifth leg. The other bulls gathered defensively behind Great Horn, but even so, they didn't cause one muscle to react outside of Carnos' easy and silent stride.

"I always enjoyed how you've led your pack, Great Horn. You, like me, have made many hard decisions that have turned out for the good, and today I present you with another. You see, my kind has enjoyed the rams, rabbits, and birds, as well as the other spoils of our land your fathers agreed never to trespass upon. But I, my brethren, and our families, like you, continue to eat more, breed more... crave more. The small animals no

31

longer fill our bellies like they used to, and we've spent many nights going to sleep while our stomachs growl to the moon in hunger. We require change, but in the spirit of our fathers, I want to propose a new treaty."

"OUT WITH IT ALREADY!" Great Horn roared so defiantly and mightily that the very air shook, causing the second-year cows to cower even further into each other. He rose to his full height and stepped so close to Carnos that their chests were now a stick apart, and their hot breath twisted into a cloud between them. If he was still scared, it didn't show, and the eldest elk was to be feared again. Carnos resisted flinching, though his sharp ears twitched, and he abandoned his wordplay.

"Fine," the wolf huffed. "I ask that you donate a dozen of your offspring to us each year so we may feast—"

"Never," Great Horn spat.

"Ten!"

"No!"

"Nine."

"I wouldn't give one! They're mine and will always be!"

"But Great Horn, it's silly to think—"

"Save your breath, Carnos," Great Horn declared for all to hear. "I wouldn't forfeit a pheasant if it crossed into our territories, the boundaries your fathers agreed to without end. We have lived many generations in peace, keeping our breeding controlled and grazing in alternating fields to avoid permanently chewing away the green. But because of *your* failure to lead *your* kin in *your* own lands, you now seek to defile an oath? No, I say, and my decision is final. Go back to where you belong, you wretched beast! Breed little and eat less for a season until the rabbits, and the rams, and all that is good becomes plentiful again, like it once was. Satisfy yourselves with what you have rather than seeking to quench your thirst in this foolish conquest. Is it not better to sleep hungry for a few moon cycles if it means sparing the blood of your own? Don't allow your kin to fall because of your ill leadership."

"ENOUGH!" Carnos growled back, equal in volume to Great Horn's shout. Turning away from the twelve, he retreated atop the boulder at the base of the slope. His calm, collected demeanor instantly vanished, and his jaw hung open as strands of saliva dripped from his lips. "Remember, elk, that I gave you a chance to save more blood than needed to be spilled. When you reflect this night, and know the tally it cost, blame your own ill leadership, for this could've played out quite differently."

Then, Carnos' neck stretched upward, his chest expanding and his neck trembling as a powerful, high-pitched howl whistled through his lips into the sky. At his signal, White Snout's hair stood on end as she heard leaves and bushes rustling from all directions, spotting wolves identical to Carnos descending the valley slope. Despite their imposing size, they slunk almost entirely silently toward them, teeth bared on either side of their mouths with tongues lolling from their gaping jaws. In a flash, all the young cows erupted into a panicked mob, screaming for their mothers as they shriveled into calves once again.

"Assemble!" shouted Great Horn. He, along with the eleven other bulls, formed a triangle, creating a barrier between the younglings and the approaching wolves as the elder cows circled the second years. "Stand fast! There's no hope unless we fend them off together."

White Snout was shoved against her peers but still managed to strain her neck to observe the bulls holding their positions, heads lowered and antlers pointed at the enemy. But, as the wolves closed the gap, one, then two, then three more pairs of amber eyes appeared over the valley's summit, descending quickly and stalking them at every turn.

Sharp's legs began to buckle. Lifting his head, he glanced back at his first pick, Round Eyes, then to White Snout, and then finally across all the second years, remembering that he was practically one of them too.

"I can't do this," he cried.

"Stand your ground, Sharp!" Great Horn spat back without moving his head to look. However, it was too late. Sharp broke free from the triangle formation and sprinted backward, nimbly jumping over some second years while tripping over others, until he escaped out the single inlet and was no longer visible. With his post deserted, a wolf lunged toward a mother elk, forcing a bull to abandon his position to defend her, quickly setting off a chain reaction that left a breach in their defense.

"Remember," Carnos taunted. "This could've been avoided."

He let out a growl and charged forward, meeting Great Horn in a clash. White Snout closed her eyes, but a multitude of sounds beat against her eardrums at once; snapping, smacking, thumping, moans, groans, howling, gurgling, and screaming—all loud and all of it unceasing. It immediately overwhelmed her senses, making her dizzy to the point that she barely heard her mother shout right next to her ear, "run if you have to!"

She wasn't sure what her mother's advice meant, but the answer revealed itself as Long Neck and the other elder cows charged forward, breaking free from their circular formation to reinforce the bulls. Now White Snout was forced to keep her eyes open to remain vigilant, compelled to watch her mother through the noise, along with the other petrified second years.

Long Neck didn't delay, dashing straight for Carnos and knocking him off Great Horn's side as he was about to bite at his exposed neck. Another wolf noticed Long Neck's brave act and used a boulder to propel himself onto her back, sinking his teeth into her shoulder. But Long Neck, quick-witted as she was, ran full force into the same boulder and twisted her body, crushing the wolf's spine against it and making him crumble to the ground. She then stomped his skull into the earth and continued to stomp until the wolf lay still in a furry heap.

This was a small victory, as more wolves appeared, pouring over the crest of the valley. It quickly became evident that this was a battle to be lost, for each one that lay still or scampered away broken and bleeding, two more came to replace it. Although every elk fought valiantly, it was impossible to fend off the continuous reinforcements now that their formations were in disarray.

White Snout contemplated her mother's advice, considering fleeing out the single inlet like Sharp had done to save his own skin. As she looked at her mother, however, her unwavering bravery inspired her. Long Neck didn't shy away when her opportunity for courage came. Perhaps she had also considered escaping, but she chose not to. Instead, she charged forward, not only for herself and her daughter but for the sake of everyone around them. As repulsive as Great Horn was, White Snout couldn't deny his wisdom; their best chance of survival was sticking together.

She didn't recognize what came over her, but amidst all the clashing noises, her next move became clear, even if foolish. She saw another wolf hanging from her mother, three on Great Horn, and the rest of the field a blur of brown and gray. She might not be able to do much, but if she could do something, even something small, the rest would have to figure itself out. Grinding her back hoof into the dirt, she lowered her head and charged toward her mother.

Though she chose this, her moment of bravery never arrived, for as she sprinted closer to the wolf attacking her mother, the ground suddenly quaked. Initially, she believed it was her own terror and excitement, her heartbeat pulsating through her extremities. But as her charge faded speedily into a trot and then eventually into a standstill, and the wolves and the elk also halted their fray, it became evident that the ground shook from something outside the valley entirely.

The elk and wolves glanced around the walls in confusion until the source of the tremor became clear.

Descending the slope was a massive brown blur, galloping toward them with others smaller in size trailing behind, dividing the foliage as they charged.

Perhaps Carnos was the first to realize what, or rather *who*, this was. He leapt atop his boulder again and howled toward the sky, "retreat! Retreat!"

The other wolves began mimicking their leader's behavior, each howling the same message so no ear would miss it. They fled toward the single inlet, away from the incoming brown streak, but not quickly enough, as a new elk emerged and joined the battlefield.

He was massive, dwarfing even Great Horn, but muscular, tall, and wide rather than sagging, slumped, and fat, and appearing no more than a few years older than Sharp. His crown of antlers boasted a dozen points on each side, spanning as wide as a tree branch and appearing as heavy as a fallen log. And his jaw, or rather the hair around his jaw, grew longer than the rest of his fur, forming an abrupt point beneath his clenched teeth. He was simply the biggest creature White Snout had ever laid eyes on, bigger than anything she had imagined possible within her own species.

Carnos leapt down from the boulder and attempted to dart away with the rest of his pack, but the new elk charged forward at full speed, catching him with an antler under his ribs. The great wolf now looked as fragile as a field rabbit as he was tossed high into the air, falling down and smacking the ground with a hard crack and a loud whimper.

"Go now, Carnos," the giant elk said. "And know that I have dealt kindly with you this day."

No further retorts came from the wolf as he lay in a heap. Dazed, he stood and immediately retracted his front right paw after attempting to put weight on it. He hobbled after the other wolves, who had already vanished.

From where this new massive elk had come, eight other cows stood in a triangle formation, all taut, tall, and muscles primed. Behind them were five other young bulls, whose faces withheld the youth of first and second years but whose bodies were larger than Sharp's. They strutted forward, out of the shrubbery, and into the small field as the two herds came face to face.

Oddly, and nearly unnoticed by White Snout, this new elk was the sole leader of his herd, which also lacked any female offspring. Though impressive in size, they were small in number for a herd.

"King Titus," Great Horn said. His face, stomach, and sides bore various bloodied lines. "I owe you my life... again."

His knees wobbled as he lowered his chest to the ground. The other bulls and cows followed his lead, and then the second years joined, until Great Horn's entire herd, including White Snout, bowed before him.

"A life owed twice is far too valuable to spend," Titus laughed. His voice was like water on a parched throat, rich, unlike any White Snout had heard, knotting her stomach. "Come now, Great Horn, stand before your king. It's times like these we must stick together to uphold the traditions of our fathers. I will not let peace fall during my reign. Tonight, allow me and my own to remain with you so that we may discuss our plan going forward. I believe *it's time*."

With a subdued groan, Great Horn righted himself from his lowered position, as did the rest of the herd. "Very wise as always, king. Let's make haste to the riverside just yonder so we can maintain watch in the open field. There, we'll discuss."

Titus nodded and was about to lead his harem alongside Great Horn's but then halted. Turning his head, his eyes fell upon White Snout, who stood all by herself, her act of charging toward her mother leaving her separated from the other second years.

"Why are you not with the others your age? Isn't this the annual Rut?" he asked.

White Snout remained quiet as her eyes momentarily darted to the ground, too afraid to move after being addressed by him, a king whose existence she'd never known until this moment. Even without the title, his very presence intimated her, for he looked as if he could snap her in half with a mild stroke of his antler.

He looked to Great Horn. "Is she yours?"

Great Horn glanced down at White Snout. "No, not mine. White Snout, return to your place among the others."

White Snout obeyed, but before she could move, Titus spoke. "White Snout? Fitting. I've never seen a cow with a white snout before. Tell me, why do you stand apart from your peers if you were not selected?"

The simple question, spoken in his rich, velvety voice, once again caused her to retreat into the recesses of her mind. A cold realization trickled in; the attention of everyone she had ever known, as well as the entirety of a new herd, was upon her. She stepped backward, the familiar urge to flee rising. She put another hoof back, then a third, and then a fourth. With each step away, she felt stranger and more awkward, painfully aware of how strange and awkward she must have seemed under the leaders' confused stares. Their inquisitive gazes made speaking impossible. Her throat tightened, and she made a noise—somewhere between a gag and a hum. She tried again, but the result was the same. Finally, she fell completely silent. She stood there, her legs trembling, as the king's question hung unanswered in the air.

To her relief, Long Neck ended the stillness. "She charged forward to protect me. A wolf was about to end my life, and she was coming to my rescue."

Titus looked to Long Neck as she strutted forward. She wasn't as strong, taut, or tall as the cows of his harem, but she carried herself with equal poise. Her back bore multiple red lines, yet she stood strong and rigid, as if untouched by injury.

"And what would someone so small have done to stop a wolf?" Titus asked, his sarcasm unmistakable.

Long Neck came shoulder to shoulder with her daughter. She glanced down, blinking hard and holding her eyelids closed a second longer than normal—just as she had when kissing her daughter back to sleep after being asked what a *wolf* truly was. "I'm not sure, but I know she would've thought of something."

Great Horn wheezed, then coughed. He was exhausted from the fight and, judging by his open mouth and half-closed eyelids, was also bored.

"Very brave," he commented dryly. "Now, White Snout, you may return to the others."

White Snout was about to move, eager to blend in once more, until Titus' voice, like before, immobilized her in her tracks.

"Yes, very brave indeed, which makes her beauty all the more memorable. I still can't believe I've never seen a white snout before."

And with that, he turned away, and together with Great Horn, he led their herds out the single inlet to a riverside, where they rested for the night.

PART III:
CALL OF THE WILD

A soft yellow light crept over White Snout's eyelids as she danced between the veil of truth and dreams. Drained by the chaos yet enchanted by sleep, she had forgotten about the wolves and their amber eyes, silent paws, and menacing fangs. She had forgotten that she'd ever charged forward when her mother was in danger, rescued by a king she'd never known before, and later questioned about her near heroism while the attention of two entirely separate herds were upon her. The memories of the valley walls, the Rut, Sharp's desertion, and any and all pains and traumas she endured had melted away while she rested, for she rested under the protection of her mother. But as she was stirred from sleep, feeling the absence of her mother's warmth, the forgotten memories slowly trickled back into her dreams until they flooded her reality.

"White Snout," her mother said, nudging her gently with her nose. "Get up."

White Snout was about to complain, still weary, but then she opened her eyes. The early dawn painted one end of the sky as the moon lingered at the other. Around her, every elk stood still, facing in one direction. Seeing she was the outlier, she quickly rose to conform with the others, unaware of what was happening but sensing its importance.

Some distance away, Great Horn stood at attention in front of Titus near the section of river where the water tumbled over the rock shelves. By their positions, Titus' harem standing stiffly behind him, White Snout inferred this was their departure. She assumed the two leaders had formed a plan to deal with Carnos, an assumption confirmed when Great Horn, and subsequently the entire herd, bowed before the king, who remained upright.

After Great Horn fought against his feeble bones to stand erect again, he hobbled back toward his own. Scanning the crowd, he furrowed his brow, and shouted, "Long Neck, where are you?"

Long Neck's back leg buckled. Looking down at her daughter, she blinked hard, her eyes glistening with a wet sheen—something White Snout had never seen before.

"Momma?" White Snout said. She moved to bump her forehead against her mother's stomach, but Long Neck withdrew as if White Snout was a strange calf from another's womb. "Momma?" she said again, her voice shrinking, her heart stung.

"Stay here," Long Neck answered coldly. She sniffed sharply to recollect herself before striding forward with her shoulders squared to meet Great Horn. When she reached him, he nodded toward Titus, and she continued on, bowing before the king as a hushed conversation began.

What's going on? White Snout thought.

Titus' throat moved frequently as he spoke, while Long Neck nodded along. Occasionally, she glanced back, easily spotting her daughter in the crowd. But whenever she did, a weird feeling crept into White Snout's stomach, the same feeling she had before the Rut, where she sensed what was happening yet remained shrouded in a thin haze of mystery.

Then, almost abruptly, Long Neck bowed again, turned, and nodded to Great Horn.

"White Snout?" he called. "Come forward."

White Snout shuddered, her heartbeat pounding so rapidly that it filled her eardrums, but her body betrayed none of it. No other elk could perceive that she was screaming inside her head or that her legs trembled in her imagination. To both herds, she appeared perfectly composed and considerably graceful as she jogged forward at the same speed as her mother, bowed before Titus like her mother had, and stood with her head held high with her mother's poise.

Standing before the king, not even he could see what truly raged within her; the worry, the distress, the anxiety, the anticipation—all tangled with the constant sense that something was about to go horribly wrong.

"You hold yourself with a subtle strength, White Snout. Even the winds seem to quiet in your presence," Titus said with a hum. His voice was raspier than the other day, the early morning playing tricks on his throat. "I'm sure you know why I summoned you."

Truthfully, she did. The circumstances clicked into place, and she understood what was about to be asked of her. Like the Rut only a day ago, her imagination stretched to meet the reality presented. Perhaps, she was becoming mature.

"I do. I only ask one thing."

He seemed amused. "And that is?"

She peered up at her mother, whose face was still as stone as she stared straight ahead. It seemed she was too afraid to allow a single muscle to quiver, lest her whole façade collapse. "I want my mother to come."

Titus drew in a slow breath, suppressing a groan. "She is claimed by another bull. Surely, you know I cannot violate this."

"But why? She's my mother," White Snout snapped, forsaking the respect due to his kingship.

"She'll go," Long Neck interrupted.

"But, momma—"

"Listen to me! I didn't raise you to be foolish. I raised you to be obedient. Now, obey me."

White Snout cowered where she stood, and this time, there were no legs to hide behind. She wanted to stomp, or headbutt her mother in the side, or scream at the top of her lungs to rouse her from this state of indifference, but her mother's face remained steadfast. Her posture was rigid, her glistening eyes fixed forward, as if something on the horizon captured her attention.

But White Snout was stubborn. She didn't care if she looked, sounded, or behaved like a calf. She wanted to be a calf again, to return to running in the fields, rolling down the mountainsides, and doing whatever felt the most fun, because her mother was protecting her. She wanted to be a first year again, before she understood the weight of consequences, before she knew what a wolf was. A cow's life was too hard. She missed being treated like she was helpless.

Despite no further communication, Titus perceived the quiet battle raging between mother and daughter, and, looking to his herd and then at Great Horn's, commanded them to disperse back to the fields.

"I'll wait across the river until you're ready," he said.

He left, and after he did, the rest of the elk resumed their respective routines, except for White Snout and Long Neck. The two stood silently next to each other, their sniffles growing louder in the silence of their unspoken argument. There was no right exchange, nothing that could mend the fracture of their bond. A small hiccup escaped White Snout, a breaking point in her resolve, and with it came a defiant stomp. She put all her strength into the ground, though it barely made an impact.

"Why would you let me go? What does he want with me?"

Long Neck's head had remained at full height since Titus stood before her, but with his absence, it finally dropped, her wet stare settling on her daughter's.

"My daughter, oh my sweet daughter." Her strong, rigid stance gave way as she leaned into her daughter, their trembling frames supporting one another. "My prayers to Freyacre have been answered. You'll be safe now."

"I don't care about being safe. I care about being with you."

"*Shhh, shhh*, I know, I know. Understand I hurt the same as you, though I do this for you."

"But, momma, I don't understand—" White Snout's throat closed, her entire chest heaving, every wave of emotion piercing her heart. She was shattered, her body wracked with pain as it craved numbness, but relief refused to come.

For a time, neither could speak. Then a gentle wind stirred, as though Freyacre itself sought to comfort them, its soft caress drying the wetness in their eyes and urging them to push forward.

"This—this isn't goodbye forever," Long Neck said, her throat trembling. She stepped away from her daughter, and although the fur around her face was a mess, a calm determination overlaid her posture. "We'll meet again at the Grove—the land of promised greens. That's where the king is taking you, where we will go too. All the elk of Freyacre will gather there, but first, you must take a separate path."

"The Grove? A separate path?" White Snout was confused. Everything felt too overwhelming to comprehend.

"You must go and alert the leaders of the other herds," Long Neck explained. "They must be warned about the wolves. Afterward, when peace reigns again, we will be reunited, never to be broken apart anymore. I promise. Until then, stay close to Titus. He'll keep you safe."

As defeated as White Snout was, she understood her mother had made this decision out of love, not because it was easy. She wanted to yell, to curse the very spirit of Freyacre, but this track had already been laid before her. As much as she might have felt like a calf, she wasn't one anymore. She was a cow, daughter of the great wolf-killer Long Neck, and perhaps that comfort would be enough to carry her until they met again.

Tough as this was, yesterday could've ended very differently if Titus never arrived—and without him, she wouldn't be standing here today. Like always, even when she hated it, her mother was right.

Channeling her courage, if not for herself then for her mother, White Snout puffed out her chest. Despite the overwhelming desire to collapse on the ground, she remained resolute, determined to present her best self for her mother to cling onto until the day she came sprinting back. Though she yearned to linger in this moment, to release the emotions weighing on her fractured heart, she couldn't bear to disappoint her mother. The decision was made, and no matter her wishes, there was no turning back.

"I will be strong, like you, momma."

"I know you will," Long Neck said.

They touched noses one last time before parting sorrowfully to join their respective harems.

In the days that followed, White Snout was broken from the soft and lax structure of her calfhood. Gone were the mornings of sleeping in as much as she desired. Instead, Una, the eldest of the other eight cows, woke her at the crack of dawn with a hard kick to the ribs. No longer did she enjoy leisurely breakfasts that could stretch into all-day feasts. Now, Titus launched into speeches about the need to save elk lives while her stomach growled, for grazing was limited to the hours before the dew dried, with the choicest greens being reserved exclusively for the bulls. In substitution of carefree afternoons of play, Titus led them on grueling treks through the fields and valleys, sparing little time for rests until nightfall. Nothing about White Snout's life felt familiar anymore, and she was constantly pushed to her limits. She feared she wouldn't be able to keep up.

Once, when White Snout's legs felt as if they might give out, she leaned against a tree, her whole body heaving for breath. And, of course, Una was there like a fly on a cut, snorting in amusement at every new discomfort White Snout endured.

"He'll leave you behind if he has to," she sneered, not a pant interrupting her steady breath. "He's done it before."

Whenever White Snout felt she couldn't take another step forward, she thought of her mother battling the wolf clinging to her side. Long Neck had killed the beast by herself, without antlers. If she could do that, then White Snout could run for her, at least until they met again— or so she hoped.

When the sun sank behind the mountaintops and the moon rose above the horizon, Titus would finally declare they form a sleep circle, with the first-year bulls taking turns patrolling the perimeter throughout the night to keep watch for predators. In the little time left before rest, she noticed the calves never played games or expressed joy in anything they did, focusing only on their duties and responsibilities.

But even in her troubles, she forced herself to remember that this was all temporary, a response to Carnos and the threat to elk territory. She could endure it if there was an end in sight—the Grove, wherever and whatever that was.

She made the mistake of asking Una what was so special about this place and immediately regretted it. The eldest cow scoffed sharply, her strength undiminished despite the wrinkles around her eyes. "I wouldn't think too much of it. You'll be lucky *if* you make it."

White Snout contemplated asking the others, but the next eldests, Secunda, Tertia, and Quarta, all shared Una's general cynicism about her. And the other cows,

Quinta, Sexta, Septima, and Octava, stayed relatively quiet, strutting away whenever White Snout approached, likely too afraid to associate with her. Even the offspring she ran alongside daily were unfriendly, wholly absorbed in the quest, their humor surfacing only when mocking their half-siblings. Everything now revolved around the task at hand, which perhaps was for the best.

White Snout was depleted at the end of each day. Although she remained curious about the Grove, at least she didn't have to pretend to be happy. She focused instead on her next breath while she ran, and on food and rest when she wasn't. To survive, she suspended herself in a trance where time seemed to vanish. This was preferable to staying grounded in her own mind, where she was constantly reminded she didn't belong among her own kind.

But her illusion would shatter whenever she was pulled back into her body, noticing how little time had actually passed. One day felt like two, two like four, and four like eight. Despite her efforts to "ignore" the wolves, the quest, and this new harem altogether, her thoughts inevitably returned to her mother. When she did come back to herself, a certain sadness resurfaced, piercing her heart like the moment she'd said goodbye. However, she clung to the belief that this separation wouldn't last forever, focusing instead on running until the moon rose, passing out from exhaustion, waking up, and repeating.

This cycle became second nature for White Snout, and after just a few days, she surprised herself when she caught sight of her reflection in a river. She looked the same; her snout was still white, and her eyes were still curious. However, she appeared more ruffled, perhaps fiercer. She was nowhere near the size of those she traveled alongside, but she was beginning to grow into her skin in her own right.

Over the span of a week, they visited three herds without any trace of Carnos, though finding a herd among the vast expanse of Freyacre proved to be a difficult challenge. During one of Titus' morning speeches, he told them that there were twelve herds in total (which White Snout connected to the number of leaders in each herd). If they kept pace according to his plan, it would take them a month to warn them all, followed by another week to reach the Grove. If White Snout could endure that, she knew her mother would be awaiting her.

On one otherwise ordinary night, with the moon and stars shining brightly behind streaking clouds, Titus cooled his body in a still pool. He wasn't far from his herd, but far enough to be considered alone. Even after traveling with him for several days, White Snout was still taken aback by his imposing size. Despite being knee-deep in water, he seemed to command the attention of the world itself. She understood why no one ever challenged his kingship over the land.

Perhaps he looked her way of his own accord, or perhaps White Snout's stare summoned his attention. In either case, their gazes met through the darkness, and he nodded ever so slightly. White Snout glanced behind her, finding no other elk in sight. She looked at him again, but he was already back to facing the sky.

"That means go to him," Una said. She was lying not far while her first-year bull, Brutus, curled against her stomach. In the moonlight, White Snout finally noticed how exhausted she looked. "Go on," she repeated glumly.

White Snout stood, her legs momentarily bending from fatigue, and slowly walked toward him. He never looked back, instead choosing to face forward, his visage consumed by the moon. As she closed the distance, she slowed her gait until her hooves were silent upon the earth. Yet somehow, he knew exactly when to speak.

"How are you faring?" he asked. She couldn't tell what he was getting at. He was always so task-oriented and commanding that to hear anything else felt disarming.

"It's... tough," she admitted. She had no reason to lie. He deserved to know what occupied her mind if he bothered to ask. After all, she did "belong" to him anyway.

"Yes, the beginning is always the toughest. You'll become accustomed to it soon."

She didn't offer a response, and neither did he elaborate. Neither did much of anything as they stood near each other in silence—him in the water, her at the edge—while the moonlight illuminated the world around them.

Eventually, he broke the stillness. "Do you know why I chose you?"

Truthfully, she had pondered this question during her runs, but at the same time, she didn't. He was a bull, and bulls chose cows they wanted to mate with, nothing more. Her own father barely paid attention to her mother unless he was in heat.

"I know, because of my white snout. You hadn't seen anything like it."

He shifted his gaze from the sky to her, and her heart skipped a beat.

"No. I admired your courage. You were ready to die if that meant saving your mother. You fought past your fear. That's a rare trait, and one I hope to pass on to my own offspring. Our stories, though years apart, are similar."

Curiosity welled up within her. "How so?"

Slowly exhaling, he briefly looked at the moon before returning his focus to her. She didn't quite understand her feelings, but having his undivided attention with no one else around felt oddly... pleasant.

"I had my initial encounter with Carnos during my first year. He wasn't much older than me, but back then, we were the same size. My mother had always told me from my earliest days that I was destined to be king and groomed me to fulfill that role. So naturally, she educated me on the traditions of our ancestors, the ways of the wild, and the Boundary, where neither elk nor wolf was to trespass. It was near the edge of my herd's lands, right where the fields went dark from the forests. I remember the elders yelling, 'stick to the open', which drove me mad. I loved the solace the shade of the trees offered from the sun, and the next forest was a great distance away.

Then one day, I saw Carnos. There he was in broad daylight, pacing back and forth across the Boundary... just watching me. I remember his teeth, the drool from his lips, and his claws digging into the dirt, threatening to pounce. They drove me insane because they were so quiet... even to my ears. As he paced, he kept taunting me, boasting how wolves were stronger and more cunning than elk until my blood boiled. Accidentally, I drifted closer and closer, and just like that, he leaned in and dragged me over."

Unbeknownst to White Snout, she leaned closer to him, the cool water now reaching her belly while he remained only knee-deep.

"He did?" she gasped.

"He did," he repeated. "Well... truthfully, I might've charged at him, but regardless, Carnos pulled me over the Boundary without crossing it, which was well within his rights. So, you see, we're not that different, though your courage is grounded in sense. I was a fool." He paused and lowered his neck for a drink. When he was done, he looked at White Snout again, her eyes and snout brightly catching the moonlight. "Admittedly, I also picked you because of your snout, but I swear that was secondary."

This sudden change in topic caught her off guard. She was so engrossed by his tale.

"What about Carnos?"

"Ah, yes." He hummed from her enthusiasm and continued. "My mother saved me just in time. She bit down on my leg as hard as she could and dragged me back to our side before Carnos could kill me. And she wasn't taking chances. She said she'd rather have a three-legged son than lose me altogether. I still have the scars beneath my fur, though they've healed fairly well."

"And your mother?" she asked. "Where is she?"

At this, his head drooped. "Gone. But she didn't die because of my stupidity. When she joined the stars, she was surrounded by loved ones... the way we all should leave this world. She taught me everything she could. I know you may not understand my ways but do understand that I know how important a mother can be. I'm not trying to take you away from yours."

White Snout sighed, remembering the sadness that had chased over the past days. "I know, the Grove. That's where I'll see her again."

He nodded. "Yes, the Grove—a fortified basin of everlasting greens known only to the highest-ranking leader of each of the twelve herds. The time has come to use it for its intended purpose, where we'll stage our defense."

Like during his morning speeches, he retreated into his mighty posture, his head reaching full height as his eyes regained their piercing intensity. For whatever reason, White Snout interpreted this as her sign to leave, for it felt more like a dismissal than an invitation for further conversation. She bowed slightly in silent gratitude for his time and began to leave.

"Where are you off to?" he asked.

"To sleep with the others," she answered.

Titus finally turned to face her, his whole body moving and leaving a small wave trailing in his wake. With the moon behind him, his form cast her in shadow, but White Snout didn't shy away. His normally rugged demeanor fell again, and his eyes grew wide, vulnerable in a way she'd never seen. In that moment, she could almost picture him, giant as he was, as a calf.

"I didn't mean to bore you. Sometimes, I forget how to speak plainly."

She nodded. "I enjoyed what you had to say."

He blinked hard, his stare settling somewhere near her eyes, clearly hesitant to meet them directly. "Forgive me for being forward. I know I'm not a romantic, but I was wondering if you'd like to… stay with me tonight. I'd love to know more about you, and I—embarrassing as it might be, feel safe around you."

He was right; he was being forward and unromantic. But there was an unmistakable kindness in his aura that intrigued her, and she would be lying if she said she didn't want to explore it further. Something deep within her found comfort in his attentiveness, even if temporary.

"Safe around me? You know I'm not exactly… fearsome." She snorted and her tail flicked playfully.

"Oh, I don't know about that," he replied, his tone softening. He tilted his head, pretending to consider her seriously. "In fact, I'm convinced you could fend off the wolves with one disapproving look. I've seen it simmer when you drift off during my morning speeches."

She giggled, but her expression twisted as she recalled the times she had nodded off from pure exhaustion, something that happened almost daily. Deciding it was best to avoid the topic, she replied with humor. "If that's all it takes, why do we need a Grove to hide in? Just send me after them."

He chuckled, clearly amused by the idea. "I must admit, I can't believe I overlooked such an apt plan. I shall require your counsel in the future." His gaze settled on the water, where the ripples stilled. His tone shifted as he spoke again, quieter, more serious. "I've observed you since our first meeting. You're untouched by the darkness that burdens so many. I'd forgotten what it feels like. I used to think my greatest comfort was the rivers, but I was thinking too big."

"Oh?" She furrowed her brow in curiosity. "What happened to the great king's love for rivers?"

He sighed, his focus turning inward. "I thought they were peaceful. When you're raised to be king, peace isn't something you're allowed to enjoy like everyone else. I was always being tested—not just by my mother, but by the bulls of each herd I came across. Because of my size, they always saw me as a threat. So I never got to be a calf, not like the others."

He paused, the moonlight glinting in his pupils. His mind momentarily flickered somewhere darker before he came to. "Those rivers were my only escape. When my legs felt worn to the bone, the water chilled my body, washing away the pain I couldn't show. I used to dream of a place of legend, where they say the water meets the horizon forever. I wanted to chase the sun and feel weightless."

White Snout watched him, taken aback by the rawness of his story. She had also heard of the legendary place from one of her half-siblings' mothers.

"It sounds foolish now, I know," he continued, almost in a whisper. "But in those moments, I could pretend I was just another calf, feeling the river's touch, free from all those eyes wanting me to fail. But maybe that was all meant to be. Without it, we might not be here. Now I've discovered a new kind of peace. It seems I've found it running through the thickets with a certain cow and her white snout."

White Snout had always felt like all she did was impede the quest with her slow pace. She finally realized what her presence meant to him, simply by being herself. "I'm glad," she replied softly.

Titus took a step closer, his antlers casting faint shadows around them. "If you stay near, I may find I no longer need places like this altogether. But tonight, I'll dream of where the water meets the horizon. It's getting late. Go join the others. I don't wish to keep you awake. I need you to listen to at least part of my speech tomorrow."

She felt a strange sensation she hadn't experienced since being with Sharp by the lake, which although not long, felt like an eternity ago. As before, her heart cracked open, and through this sliver, she recognized the beauty of the moment. She was chosen by a king, the leader of leaders, who didn't seek to steal her away from her mother but to protect her from the wolves that had come so close to ending her life. He was, in every respect, a gentle and kind elk who desired what was best for her and her kind. She began to see, perhaps, what he had known all along.

"I—" Just as when he addressed her in front of her calfhood herd, she had to fight through her closing throat. But being alone with him, with his wide eyes solely on her, it became a bit easier. "I wouldn't mind staying close to you this night."

He hummed, a flicker of disbelief crossing his face before gently, almost reverently, lowering his head to press his snout against her forehead, as if ensuring the moment was real.

PART V:
ANCESTORS FROM AFAR

Autumn's spell tightened its grip over the land in the coming days as the spirit of Freyacre prepared for its season of rest. In the mornings, a delicate layer of ice clung to the river's edge, melting away with the afternoon sun, while the grass shifted from brittle to supple, and back to brittle as the day wore on. Every breeze carried a sharper chill than the last, and the once-vibrant leaves turned from fiery hues to brown, then darker still, before detaching from their stems and blanketing the forest floor. However, the spirit of Freyacre was a generous one, offering its final gifts of the year in the form of acorns, seedlings, berries, and mushrooms to sustain its inhabitants through the harshest of winters. Though everything in White Snout's world grew colder, the warmth of the king's affection kept her heart aflame.

During Titus' morning speeches, if she were to catch his eye, his typical commanding demeanor would slip into his full, round eyes. While they ran, she challenged herself to keep pace alongside him, bumping playfully into his side with her snout before bounding away in a fit of mirth. She had a knack for piercing his hardened veneer, and he couldn't resist the thrill of tackling her into a heap of leaves whenever the chance arose.

Titus allowed his harem and calves more frequent rests than they were accustomed to, using this time to share quiet conversations with White Snout, revealing glimpses into his wistful thoughts. Each night, despite having eight other cows in his harem, he kept her closer than the rest.

This favoritism didn't go unnoticed, especially by Una. Whenever White Snout drifted far enough from Titus to be out of his earshot, Una would seize the opportunity to needle her with doubts, provoking her to second-guess her place among them.

"He loved all of us at one point," Una once said. "Enjoy it while he cares. Next year, we'll both be watching him favor another."

White Snout tried to dispel these remarks. She convinced herself she was different from the other cows in his harem. She was demure when he led the herd, yet nurturing when they were alone and he was vulnerable. She hadn't seen any other cow, or offspring for that matter, make him as happy as she did, where his whole chest heaved with genuine delight. But still, Una's voice resonated within her and gnawed at her further when her troupe—Secunda, Tertia, and Quarta—chimed in with their snickering. The three of them loved echoing Una's insults.

"I remember when he was all about *me*. He couldn't keep himself from mounting me every chance he got. Feels just like yesterday," Secunda gushed during a run.

"What a beast he is... when he wants to be," Tertia snorted.

"Oh, stop making me jealous," Quarta said. "You're making me almost miss him."

Despite White Snout's best efforts, she couldn't prevent these comments from unraveling her fragile happiness. When she wasn't with him, which was more often than not, she was surrounded by the rest, who clearly viewed her as an outlier. After all, she hadn't been with them long. He had entire lives with these cows and had to have loved—or at least enjoyed—them at some point, and his offspring were a blatant reminder of that.

Although she was a second year, the five first-year bulls still dominated her in size. When they ran together, she felt as slow as a sheep, and even though she trained just as hard as they did, during each rest, she was the only one panting and desperate for a sip of water.

I belong with them, she forcefully reminded herself. *I'm just as good as any.*

During the day, she felt like a stranger, but at night, lying beside Titus, she no longer questioned where she belonged. Whenever their eyes met, the sting of the other cows' insults melted away. Whenever she bumped into his side and he chuckled, she forgot about her petite frame. Whenever they conversed, she felt like the only cow that mattered to him. And she was positive he felt the same way.

Each night, the first question Titus would ask was how she was faring, and each night, she answered honestly. She told him it was difficult. She told him about the insults, how her legs constantly trembled and ached, and how she felt like she didn't belong except when he was near. His heart and eyes remained open as he listened, affirming her feelings with constant nodding and the occasional brush of his jaw against her neck. Whenever doubt overcame her and reflected in her expression, he would lean in, whispering the same line that reliably erased all worries from her heart.

"You are my beloved. Only you. Don't forget that."

When they entered the fourth week of their quest and had alerted only nine out of the twelve herds about Carnos and his pack, they encountered a mountain that stretched as far as the eye could see in either direction. To say it was steep would diminish its dominance over the neighboring peaks, turning their daily runs through fields and valleys into an exhausting uphill slog.

White Snout, though much stronger now since joining Titus, simply couldn't push forward against the incline. Her legs felt as delicate as blades of grass, ready to bend and buckle with each uphill step. Exhaustion dulled her other senses, leaving her head spinning and vision blurred. Her hooves fell carelessly into the furrows of the path and threatened injury. Naturally, she had fallen to the back of the herd, and the thick shrubbery made it difficult to track everyone else. But somehow, intentionally or not, Una was never far off, always there to relish the newcomer's struggle.

"He'll leave you behind if he has to. We all will," she reminded coarsely.

White Snout was tired of the chatter and too weary to hold her tongue.

"Be quiet," she snapped. "You're just bitter that he loves me more than you."

The elder cow scoffed. "Love? Ha, what is that? Without peace, there's only survival."

"That's not true," White Snout said. Although she felt right in her conviction, she also felt like a calf for vocalizing it.

"Oh, you don't believe me, little one? Tell me, have you seen death? And not the kind where one falls asleep to join the stars, but when life is ripped from their throat, limbs picked apart as easily as we eat leaves? How they lick their lips at just the thought? No? I thought so. Only then will you realize *everything* is about survival."

White Snout tried to ignore her but failed. Una never offered anything of value to her, so why should she listen now? Instead, she grunted, and although her legs burned with every slight progression, she pressed forward. But even with her new determination, her hoof got caught in a small pile of pebbles, and she slipped, her chest smacking the ground before she could catch herself.

"Pitiful," Una said. "You're better off—"

"Enough!" Titus roared. From the shrubbery, his massive body divided the path as his kind eyes settled on the fallen cow. "Una, this is harsh, even for you. Have the years wiped away your compassion?"

Una huffed. "Compassion? Don't sicken me by pretending you care. She's just another one of your playthings."

"Una—"

"But, Titus, you know this to be true. I know you better than that."

At this, the five first-year bulls poked their curious heads above the shrubbery, followed by the other seven cows. Much like during Titus' morning speeches, the entire herd was involved in this moment, every word reaching every ear. Una's eyes began to glisten, and Titus, rather than yelling again, chose to stand silent.

"You ever wonder why, *White Snout*, there are only male offspring? Did that ever cross your tiny, diminutive mind, *hmmm*?"

White Snout couldn't tell if she was being genuine or deliberately dramatic, but in either case, she didn't have to look around to realize... Una was right.

"Not now, not like this," Titus pleaded, but Una stomped her hoof and glared so fiercely that even the young bulls cowered in place.

"It's because he leaves the newborn females with other herds, so they don't impede his 'leadership training'. I've had four of my own ripped away from my teat, given to strangers where I was forced to believe that they'd be raised with a sliver of the love I could've provided. And why, why did I do that? Because I trust Titus, because he knows what's at stake.

Did you ever wonder why my name is Una? And hers is Secunda, and hers Tertia, and hers Quarta?" She nodded to the others. "Because if we were attacked, we need to be reminded that we function as a hierarchy to maintain the greater good of all elk. And I do this—I obey my king's every command because I was his first. Out of every possibility in Freyacre, he chose me as his partner, and I accepted proudly knowing the consequences. Not *you*, not anyone else! Me!

But now, he throws every rule to the wind with you. Let's eat more. Let's rest more. What's so special about you anyway?" The eldest glared at the youngest. "Tell me, Titus. Why is she allowed to keep her name? It should be Nona, as tradition commands. Is it because of her white snout? Please, don't tell me you're that weak. She's no more special than we are. Or do you think otherwise, my king? Will she be allowed to raise a cow too, should she give birth to one? Granted, she doesn't die first. She's far too fragile to bear a calf from your lineage."

White Snout looked at Titus, who remained still, and was unsure of her emotions. She had fallen for him, or so she thought. Yet, in this moment, she couldn't shake the question—who was he? She wanted to believe these accusations weren't true, but the pieces fit together all too well. Why did he appear sheepish as he stood before his herd when he was mightier than them all? And so, she asked him in a near whisper, almost afraid of the answer, "is this true?"

Their gazes locked, and for a second, his eyes widened as if they were alone before narrowing into something unreadable. When he spoke, his bearing was cold and detached, unlike anything she had witnessed before.

"We lay here tonight. Be ready on the 'morrow."

The sun still hung high above, with much of the day yet to wane before the moon would rise. Yet, no one questioned his decision, not even Una. He turned and strode uphill to a rock ledge, where he settled, overlooking them and the valley below.

The rest of the elk remained immobile for some time, as though the first to move would incur his wrath. But once one finally did, it broke the tension and eased the others. Even so, they didn't converse louder than a whisper for the rest of the evening.

While it was still dark, White Snout was met with a hard nudge to the side.

"Get up," she heard, but not from Una, as she was accustomed. She peeled back her eyelids to see Titus standing over her. He appeared alert, his muscles taut, and not a blink of weariness apparent.

"Titus, what's wrong?" she said softly. In the early morning and with added sleep, she had forgotten that she was ever troubled by him.

"Be ready, Nona. We leave soon," he said back.

Her jaw slid open, and she tilted her head, attempting to discern meaning behind this cold façade, for she had done nothing wrong. Yet, she felt nothing, his heart no longer within her unique reach. With each blink of clarity, she remembered the night before; how he had kept himself distant from the others, still within eyesight, but far enough away to avoid anyone's company. Who was this elk standing before her, so distant from the one she thought she knew?

He trotted around to the others in ascending order, rousing each from their slumber with a hard nudge from his hoof. Even Una looked disturbed when she was forced awake last.

"What's the meaning of this? The moon still shines."

Ignoring her, he surveyed his harem and calves to ensure all were awake and attentive before positioning himself at the head of their sleep circle.

"We still must alert three herds on the other side of the mountain before we can make way for the Grove, and we must no longer delay. Carnos and his kind have been trailing us."

"How do you know?" gasped Tertia.

Titus nodded to a bush near their perimeter, and Brutus sprinted to the spot. He moved the bush with his antler nubs, and there, plainly visible to all, was Carnos' large, five-pointed print in the mud.

"The front made less of an impression than the rest," Titus said. He looked to his first years. "Which means?"

All the young bulls stepped back, except for Brutus, who didn't notice the cue. "That... uh—he's still injured?" he squeaked.

"Good elk," Una said, praising her son.

Titus peered around at them all, except for White Snout, whom he deliberately passed over. Then, with a distinguished bugle, he shouted, "Carnos, your tracks are still wet. Reveal yourself now, or let this day mark you as a coward forever."

Silence answered him.

"As I thought." He then lowered his voice to address his own. "I want to apologize to you all for my recent behavior. My leadership has grown slack during the reign of peace we've enjoyed. That time will come again, but for now, we are on a quest that shapes our very future. We will wake up earlier and sleep later. We will succeed at any cost and reach the Grove. As king, I swear this to you."

White Snout glanced again at the print in the mud, its size as big as her head.

"Una," Titus said.

"Yes," she answered.

"Tonight, you will lie closest to me, as the hierarchy commands."

From the corner of her eye, she glanced at White Snout, a wry expression creeping over her face.

"It shall be so, my king," she answered proudly.

Titus nodded. "Cows, graze while you can. And bulls?"

The five younglings stiffened their posture.

"Not a twig shall pass your lips until noon. It matters not who failed in keeping the night's watch, for we rise and fall together. Each of you must bear the weight of responsibility. Thank the stars you're still standing with us."

Despite the punishment, the bulls dared not utter a complaint. Titus surveyed them once more, squinted again at the wolf print, then up at the mountain's crest. They were only a third of the way up, with the steep climb ahead promising no relief. Finally, he lifted his gaze toward the expansive sky, where a lone star defiantly pierced the encroaching sunrise.

"Thank you, mother, for watching over me," he said. "I won't let you down again."

PART VI:
NONA, THE NINTH BRIDE

B y nightfall, they reached the mountain's summit, and the following day, descended to its opposite base. At the end of the third day, luck was on their side when they found one of the three remaining herds idling at the edge of a field beneath the shade of some canopy. Titus, as he had with Great Horn, warned the leader about the wolves, instructed the herd to make way for the Grove, and departed at dawn toward the final two herds.

During this, White Snout found no chance to speak with him, not in the way she had before. Their words were sparse, and on the rare occasion they did speak, it was always about something shallow; eating, sleeping, or urging her to run faster, as if she wasn't already doing her best. It was nothing like the idle conversations she had come to cherish in the brief time they'd spent together. She tried to endure the ache from the sudden lack of affection but failed in every endeavor. Her mind conjured excuses for his coldness, for her heart still yearned for him.

Yes, he had changed her name, surely out of tradition, she convinced herself, not from any ill will toward her.

It was the same reason he left the newborn females with other herds; a responsibility dictated by his position. He was king after all, and being king came with sacrifices she hadn't fully understood—and might never fully grasp. She was still new to all of this. Before she could speak with him alone, she resolved to withhold judgment. Buried beneath his hardened veneer lay a gentle and kind elk she had come to know. She had witnessed this side of Titus on countless occasions and had been fortunate enough to share in his happiness. Though the days were difficult, she clung to the intimate memories of when they were truly together—when he wasn't confined by his role as king, when he'd whisper so sweetly into her ear, "you are my beloved. Only you. Don't forget that."

Those three lines kept him alive in her heart and gave her the strength to face every obstacle in her path. If her body couldn't keep up with the relentless pace, then perhaps her spirit could. And if nothing else, she reminded herself to survive for her mother.

Nine grueling days had crawled by since they spotted Carnos' print, and now only one herd remained to be warned. It was on this morning that Titus finally addressed White Snout during his speech.

"Nona, tonight, you shall lie closest to me."

At another time, the mere thought of this honor would have made her swoon. But she knew he was simply upholding tradition according to rank. It was fair, she supposed, but her heart wished he would set aside the expectations of king and act on his true desires, if he still had any. Her mind swirled with questions she longed to ask. Yet, she doubted she could break through his hardened shell even if they were alone, or that his answers would satisfy her. All she could do was endure the anguish for a little longer and survive the waiting.

The afternoon leading up to their night together stretched long and cold. The chill, if nothing else, helped numb her legs. They still burned on the roughest parts of the trek, but it was nothing compared to the pain of her earliest days with the herd. When the hour finally came for them to be together, her nerves rose with the thought of being near him. She stopped by a river to gulp down its icy water, hoping to calm her trembling. When she returned to the herd, she found him already settled at the base of a great oak. A vacant spot beside him awaited her.

She came to his side and folded her legs, sinking into the ground with a stifled sigh. Despite the cold, his body radiated warmth like its own sun, chasing away the chill the moment she drew near. She nestled into his fur, resting her head just beside his mouth. Though this was their designated time, and the others weren't far off, she whispered, hoping to keep their conversation a secret.

"Titus?"

Despite having rehearsed many conversations in her head, she found she couldn't bear to be cross with him, at least not yet. He lifted his head, meeting her gaze. At first, his eyes were narrow, guarded, but in a few fleeting seconds, his pupils quivered and softened.

"White Snout," he breathed. Leaning into her, he pressed his head close until their necks intertwined. "I've missed you."

"I missed you too," she replied, her anger, confusion, worry, and distress evaporating like dew beneath the morning sun. Yet even as relief flooded her, one question refused to leave her mind.

"Please, tell me Una wasn't telling the truth," she implored.

He turned away though his face remained soft.

"It is. The traditions were set by our forefathers, not me. Even Great Horn follows a path, just like the rest of the leaders. And though it's not my doing, I understand why they had to enact such strict rules. If I fall by the teeth of a predator due to my carelessness or my failure to uphold what I swore to protect, how would any of the twelve herds keep faith? It's exactly times like these that prove why such standards exist. I follow a track set long before me, one I can no longer stray from, not by my choice, but because it was chosen for me. When peace reigns once more, I swear to you, what you endure now will be but a fading dream. Then, we will be together again, properly, like we were before. No more running every day or masking our affection."

A brief silence settled between them as his words lingered in the cold night air. Eventually, she nodded, her heart finding a fragile solace in his promise. The fear that the Titus she believed in was nothing more than a figment of her imagination began to fade. His presence, where he *felt* near, grounded her, washing away the illusion Una's words had tried to create.

"Just promise me something," she said, breaking the quiet.

"What is it, little one?" he asked.

76

She squirmed, a hint of discomfort in her movements. "Promise you won't leave me behind."

His head jerked back slightly, his shock evident. "Leave you behind?" he repeated, his tone laced with disbelief. "I'd never."

Her voice wavered as she pressed on. "Una said you have before."

A shadow of frustration crossed his face, but his voice remained calm. "No, no, I can assure you that's not true. She lies because she's jealous. I'll tell her to stop spreading rumors. It lowers morale."

White Snout didn't know what else to say, though she trusted him. She might not have when she was an oblivious calf rolling down the hillside, but those days were far behind her. She had seen Carnos and the dozens of wolves that followed them, a sight that had shaken her understanding of the world. While still somewhat ignorant, she was beginning to grasp the vast gap in knowledge that only years of experience and leadership could fill. But she was willing to learn, willing to embrace the role of a cow who supported her king. As Great Horn had once said, if he had offered any useful advice; "we must band together to fend off danger."

All the questions and accusations that had pervaded her mind in recent days now seemed trivial beneath the weight of Titus' gaze. She had more to learn and experience, but she refused to let those uncertainties chew away at what little time she had with him. The journey had left her weary, her legs aching and her spirit stretched thin. Perhaps another hour wouldn't pass before exhaustion claimed her. Every second with him was precious.

She went to nudge him, but he pulled back, his sudden withdrawal sending a pang through her chest. Her lips trembled.

"What's wrong?" she whispered.

He stared out into the distance, yet she felt his heart remain open to her.

"I brought you into my harem without explaining the responsibilities that came with it. I let my infatuation get the best of me and made the decision for you in haste. I've lacked discipline in these recent times, and perhaps, if it wasn't for Carnos, I would've forgotten it completely." He swallowed hard, his voice dropping lower. "What I'm trying to say is... once we arrive at the Grove, you can rejoin your mother's herd if you like... permanently. I won't bind you to an oath you didn't accept on your own terms. This is my folly, and the decision lies with you."

This struck her to the core. Never had she encountered such kindness and respect from an elder bull, let alone a king. She had been raised by the twelve leaders of her herd, strong and valiant like Great Horn, but all shared a certain aloofness in their mannerisms. Even her father, though she knew he cared, had been mostly absent during her upbringing, his time divided among many cows and offspring.

Perhaps with a reign of peace came the reign of foolish leaders. Her mother, though the strictest of her herd's cows, had not passed down many of the teachings she herself retained. White Snout was allowed to wake up whenever the sunlight forced her eyelids open. She was permitted to run up hills and roll back down under her mother's watchful eye, yes, but often beyond the immediate protection of the bulls. She was lavished with luxuries and indulged in lazy habits, the kind that could only flourish when danger wasn't truly a concern.

Since then, in what felt like a blink of an eye, her life had been drastically reshaped, her very nature altered by the harsh realities she had faced. Peace would return one day, she clung to that hope, but until then, they had to fight for it. And fighting meant supporting the king, upholding tradition, and standing firm against the trials they faced. If her efforts, no matter how small, could lighten the burden on his shoulders, she would give them willingly.

"Titus," she said. Finally, he looked back at her, and although his gaze settled upon her, no fear constricted her throat, for she trusted him completely. "You are my beloved *throughout time*. Only you. Don't forget that."

A shiver rippled up his spine, his hair standing on end as her words settled over him. She had held onto his promise just like he had instructed, adding her own slight variant, a reminder that no gap in age could sever the bond between them, and he was visibly taken aback by the depth of its impact. He reached for her with his neck, mindful of his antlers, and nibbled at her ear, his hot breath forming a cloud around her chest, warming her against the frigid air.

"Let's get further away from the others, just for a little while. My bulls will keep watch over them. They should be extra vigilant this night."

Her heart thrummed in her chest, and after they both quietly stood, she trotted closely behind him as he led her behind the veil of nearby shrubs. Here, she delighted in the chance to be alone with him, reminiscent of the beginning when it felt unburdened, intimate, and unspokenly theirs.

PART VII:
FORBIDDEN FOREST

As White Snout was gently caressed awake, she was met by Titus' soft gaze, his antlers stretching beyond her vision and his normally pointed beard curling under his chin. For a fleeting moment, she was unaware that she had awoken, for he was everything she dreamed. She didn't realize she was awake until he leaned in, planted his lips against her forehead, and whispered, "rise, White Snout, my beloved *throughout time*."

She obeyed, and standing, was reminded of how sore she was, not just from the grueling days of running, but also because of a night well spent with him. But no ache could make her regret their time together. If anything, she yearned to be alone with him again, where the world faded into bliss, and he became her everything.

"I'll hold onto our memories. Until next time," he said in a tender hush. Then, his stare hardened as he resumed the mantle of king, going about waking the others, except for Otho, Tertia's bull, who had kept watch during the last hour.

"Arise, my herd," he called out.

Once they all shook themselves awake from their huddled slumber, they lined up before him, as they had done every morning thus far, awaiting his speech.

"We know the quest. We know what to do. There's one herd left, and then to the Grove." His voice carried the weight of purpose, but his expression lightened slightly when his gaze landed on White Snout, and a suppressed hum escaped him. "Be cheery with me, my fellow elk, for the end is in sight. Let us graze extra to put meat on our bones to brace for the weather. And cows, if you discover a bitterbrush before the bulls, it's yours to keep." He stepped back, about to dismiss them, when Una's sharp stomp jogged his memory. "Oh, and Una, you will accompany me this night."

"My pleasure, king," she replied, her tone icy.

Like in the beginning, White Snout easily captured her beloved's attention without seeking it out. During the day's run, his gaze would often linger on her unexpectedly, even on nights he spent with other cows. Each time she caught him staring, warmth bloomed in her chest, and she giggled silently, secure in the knowledge that his love for her was steadfast.

Naturally, he allowed his strictness to ease once more—at first, just a few extra minutes of grazing here and there, then longer rests during the run, and finally, a bit more sleep. Yet he reassured the herd that these allowances were for their benefit, not due to any laxness on his part. The days were growing colder, and the nights were harsher. With greens becoming scarce, he insisted the extra time was necessary for foraging. It wasn't untrue, but much of this so-called "time for foraging" he spent with White Snout.

Although one herd remained to be warned before their journey to the Grove, Titus often declared each morning that their quest was practically over. Despite the snow creeping further down the mountains and the ground hardening with each dawn, his delight in their progress was unmistakable. It was hard to tell whether his joy stemmed from his time with White Snout or the nearness of the Grove. And was it wrong that White Snout believed him?

If he wasn't concerned, why should she be? Titus was the mightiest elk in all Freyacre. She had seen him face off against Carnos, tossing the wolf through the air with a flick of his antlers. If he could do that so effortlessly, surely he could fend off an entire wolf pack if it came to that, especially with the support of his well-trained cows and bulls. Together, they were superior to any force in Freyacre. So instead of worrying about limping Carnos, who had likely lost their trail by now, she shifted her focus to something far more enticing; her next night with Titus. Each day became a countdown.

Una's night came and went, followed by Secunda's, then Tertia's. Quarta's turn passed, then Quinta's, Sexta's, and Septima's. The eighth night would be Octava's, but finally, on the ninth, it would be White Snout's, her world revolving around that thought. And although her sole concern was running after Titus, it was becoming clear it wasn't for the other cows.

They had spent over a week searching for the last herd to no avail; no hoofprints, scat, or any markers to suggest where they ought to be. Titus reassured them they must be close, unless the missing elk had strayed from their designated territory. Such a thing, however, was forbidden by elk tradition, and so he declared it to be an impossibility. Yet their five-week quest was now entering its seventh. Initially, Titus was too distracted by White Snout to let his anxiety take root, but as their night together neared and the elusive herd remained unfound, his apprehension began to show.

While they scoured the land for the last herd, Titus stopped at a river while the sun was at its peak to take a break. Rather than drinking or grazing on the sparse grass, he stood motionless, his attention fixated on a distant stretch of woods.

White Snout noticed his tension and approached him, whispering softly, "what is it, my love?"

He didn't move, his eyes darting from side to side, scanning the trees and shadows. "No... they couldn't have. Could they?"

At this, Una's ears perked. She trotted to Titus' side, nudging White Snout aside with a firm shoulder and asking the same question in a tone far more commanding. "What is it, my king?"

Her sharp voice snapped him back into his skin with a shiver, and he realized a few more curious elk ears had perked toward them.

"It's just... absolutely not. Elk must never venture into *that* forest. That'd be reckless."

He muttered a curse under his breath and, without further explanation, strode toward the forest's edge. The biting cold didn't seem to faze him as he waded knee-deep into the icy river, his steps purposeful and unyielding.

White Snout hesitated until the rest of the herd strode in after him. The freezing water rose to her belly, its chill seeping into her bones with each careful step. Amidst the discomfort, an ominous sensation gripped her chest, distinct from the frigid embrace of the water. As she waded onward, the familiar pine scent of Freyacre was tainted by a sharp, sickly sweetness, sharp and foreign. It twisted her stomach, and though she still couldn't discern Titus' intentions, she felt the shift in the air—a creeping unease that seemed to emanate from the forest ahead.

"Tertia?" White Snout asked, her voice barely above a whisper as they plodded through the icy river. "What did he mean by *that* forest?"

Tertia hesitated, her usual guard faltering in the face of the ominous atmosphere. Relinquishing their rivalry, she leaned closer. "The Boundary is in that forest. Look at the trees."

As they exited the river and drew nearer, what had seemed like an ordinary forest began to morph in White Snout's eyes. The trees bore strange carved lines along their bark, reminiscent of velvet-shedding marks made by bulls. Unlike the occasional scarred tree she was used to, these markings adorned every trunk that lined the forest's edge, as if by design. The fading hues of autumn, slowly yielding to winter's stark palette, framed the scene, but one color stood out, a deep crimson streak smeared across the bark of the nearest tree.

White Snout's gaze lingered on the mark, and the air grew heavier with every breath she took. The scent it carried, subtle at first, grew cloying with each gust of wind. It wasn't the familiar sweetness of blackberries, she realized, but something far more sinister. Her eyes darted from Titus to the other cows, all standing silent and still. In their tight expressions and pinned-back ears, she saw the same terrible thought rising within her. A sickening taste spread across her tongue as nausea climbed her throat.

That mark carried no scent of fruit. It carried the sharp, biting tang she remembered from cuts inflicted by thorn bushes, from the time Sharp had gored Broadhoof's forehead, and from the wolves' claws raking across her mother's skin. Her stomach twisted violently, and she trembled, her legs rooted as if frozen by the weight of the truth. Her mind raced with the same chilling question Titus had uttered before.

They couldn't have... could they?

Titus' back leg twitched in a sharp, instinctive motion. Then, with his chest puffed and his resolve clear, he galloped at full speed into the woods. Though unspoken, the herd knew their role; to form their protective triangle and wait patiently unless summoned by his bugle.

Time crept by under the watchful sun, and no one moved a muscle or uttered a word. Every ear strained to catch the faintest sound, every eye fixed on the shifting shadows of the forest. The trees loomed, their thick trunks masking the forest's depths. The herd knew that if a threat emerged, they would have only moments to react.

The tension heightened with a sudden snap of a twig, followed by the rustling of a nearby bush. The first-year bulls stepped forward instinctively, but the mother cows quickly shoved them back, positioning them near White Snout. Every leg in the herd stiffened, ready to spring into action, as something barreled out from between the trees.

But alas, it wasn't an enemy. It was Titus.

He emerged, his steps heavy and uneven. His expression was hollow, the fire within him snuffed out. His spirit, so commanding just hours before, now was distant, absent.

"Survivors?" Una asked, breaking the silence. Somehow, she still sounded composed.

Titus ignored her, his focus elsewhere. His trot slowed to a halt before the herd. His head sank low to the ground, his eyes still glinting faintly with emotion. His jaw and throat vibrated in a rhythmic tremor, pausing briefly before the motion repeated. After the third cycle, he unleashed a bugle so powerful it seemed to shake the very trees, sending startled birds scattering from their nests into the sky.

At first, the sound carried a somber beauty, a ceremonial mourning for the lost herd. But the grief quickly gave way to fury as Titus thrashed his antlers wildly in a circle, slamming them repeatedly into the ground.

"How stupid can they be!" he roared. "They know better!"

Una abandoned her place at the head of the triangle formation and stepped into action. She directed the cows and bulls to recross the river and establish a sleep circle, her calm authority cutting through the chaos. It was a break from tradition for a cow to take command, but tradition had little relevance in their current predicament.

As Titus continued to spin and strike his antlers against the earth, Una approached him cautiously. She began to sing, her low, soothing voice weaving a melody that flowed through the crisp air like a gentle current. White Snout did not leave with the others. She remained steadfast with Una, rooted to the spot where she had stood since Titus first disappeared into the forest. Her eyes stayed fixed on him, her heart heavy with both sorrow and resolve as the king wrestled with his grief.

"What do you want?" Una snapped, sensing White Snout's lingering presence without having to glance back. "Can't you see I have enough to handle right now?"

"It's just…" White Snout began, her voice faltering as she watched her beloved thrash in anguish. Her heart ached to rush to his side, to comfort him with a gentle nuzzle, but his wild movements and fury held her at bay. Her gaze drifted to the crimson streak on the nearby tree, and her stomach twisted at the thought of the horrors he must have faced beyond the forest's edge. Yet her longing to support him, to be with him in his most vulnerable moment, overpowered her fear.

"I know. Tonight's your turn with him," Una answered on behalf of White Snout. This was far from

White Snout's mind, but she chose not to correct her. The eldest glared back at the youngest, her eyes gleaming in the sunlight as well. "Wait until tomorrow. You wouldn't know how to deal with this."

Despite her inner turmoil, White Snout surrendered. She felt utterly helpless in the face of Titus' distress. Comforting him when he was merely troubled had always felt natural, but this depth of devastation was uncharted territory for her. Though her heart ached to be by his side, their connection seemed distant now, his spirit ensnared by the horrors he had encountered in the forest.

Reluctantly, White Snout acknowledged her limitations and deferred to Una's wisdom. Experience outweighed desire in moments like these, no matter how deeply she longed to help. She could only hope that time would ease Titus' anguish. If not, she resolved to do all she could to lift his spirits when they were together on the morrow. Her love for him left her no choice—it compelled her to try, even if success seemed impossible.

PART VIII

KING OF HEARTS

T hat very night, the wind howled across the plains, forests, valleys, mountains, rivers, and lakes as the first snowflakes of winter descended to the lowest reaches. The spirit of Freyacre had fallen into a deep slumber for the remainder of the year, leaving Titus' herd huddled together for warmth beneath a lone tree in an expansive field. Even the night's lookouts, Jovian, Sexta's first-year bull, and Manius, Quinta's, kept watch for danger from their mothers' sides, having convinced Titus that patrolling the perimeter, as customary, would surely leave them frozen to death.

Being the newest addition to the harem, or perhaps because she was the least liked, White Snout was forced to the outer ring, where only Octava's back provided her with any body heat, leaving her other half exposed to the bitter cold. Titus slept snugly in the middle, surrounded by his harem and calves with Una nestled beside him— where White Snout belonged, for it was the ninth night.

With the discovery of the last herd's fate, their running ended abruptly while the sun still lingered in the sky. White Snout tried to convince herself that the reserved energy was keeping her awake, but deep down, she knew better. Whenever she closed her eyes, she saw the dark red streak on the tree bark and smelled the acrid sweetness that twisted her stomach. As she drifted asleep, her imagination led her deeper into that harrowing forest, where blood bathed the ground and tufts of brown fur floated in the air. Images of wolves flaying skin from flesh, flesh ripped from bone, and bone cracked by teeth flashed so vividly against her eyelids, and the phantom echoes of howls and screams grew so deafening, that each time they crescendoed, she jolted awake with her heart thrumming wildly in her chest and a scream choking in her throat.

When she jerked from this half-sleep, she reminded herself it was simply her mind playing tricks on her, though her imagination mirrored the true demise of the twelfth herd. Her own calfhood herd would have suffered the same end had Titus not been there to save them. She silently thanked Freyacre for giving her a hero like him to protect her.

Each time her terrors spooked her awake, she would lift her head and peer over the sides of the other elk, spotting him at the center. He was so beautiful and majestic, for while he rested, all his distress faded, softening the king's rigid shell and leaving him at ease, like when they were alone. She could almost forget the cold sweeping against her back and the cows' taunts, because tomorrow, she'd be the one nuzzled under his warm chin.

Thanks to Titus, she laughed away the wolves that haunted her dreams—at least while she was awake.

Whenever she nodded off again, the confidence she placed in the king dissipated along with her reasoning. The blood on the tree beckoned her back into the forbidden forest, where terrors preyed on her imagination like a soft-winged owl on a mouse.

After one, two, then three failed attempts to doze off, she awoke once more, her stomach exuding heat despite her fur being speckled with snow. She gazed up at the stars and then at the swollen moon, wondering briefly if her mother might be looking at them too. Now that their quest to alert the herds was complete, well—to their best, it wouldn't be long before they were reunited.

Strangely, since joining Titus, her love for him made everything feel both achingly slow when they were apart and impossibly fast when they were together, though right now, she was in the slow part. She stretched her neck, craning her head over Octava's side to catch another glimpse of her beloved's face. To her surprise, she found him awake this time... and so was Una.

Their snouts were so close they nearly touched, necks practically intertwined, and their throats trembled with muted conversation. No matter how hard White Snout strained her ears, the whistling wind drowned their voices. Yet she didn't need to hear Titus's words; his bearing spoke volumes. His shoulders were relaxed, leaning forward slightly with his head lowered so that he could look into Una's face. His eyes were wide and soft, the same way they were when he was alone with her. Though her heart rose to see his spirits renewed, a pang of jealousy gnawed at her to know another cow could do this—especially Una.

White Snout lowered her head and wedged herself tighter against Octava's back, shutting her eyes in an effort to forget what she'd just seen. Yet questions needled her mind, refusing to let her rest. How could Una soothe his heart as she did? What could they possibly be discussing so late into the night? And most troubling of all; did Una truly know him better, and therefore love him, in a way she never could?

Impossible, she thought. But then again, was it? White Snout was still a second year, while Una had known him from the beginning. She tried vainly to push these chittering thoughts from her mind, guilt welling up behind them. Mothers, fathers, and calflings had suffered the most excruciating pain, and here she was, jealous because he acted happy? *How could I be so selfish*, she berated herself. *Like a spoiled calf. Ridiculous.*

And yet, peace evaded her entirely as she lay there. The gnawing pull of curiosity pricked at her again, louder than her guilt or exhaustion. Rest was already elusive, stolen by her nightmares, or so she reasoned. She raised her head, unable to resist spying on him once more.

She carefully stood in a crouch. With her knees bent and head lowered, she remained hidden behind the rest of the cows, curled in a ball on their sides. Silently, she circled the outskirts of the huddle, tactfully avoiding Jovian and Manius's bleary-eyed watch as they nodded in and out of sleep. When she reached the opposite side of the lone tree, she was only half a step closer to Titus than before, but now she was downwind. The chilled gusts carried the once muted hum of their conversation to her prying ears.

"—as if it was yesterday," Titus whispered to Una. "There were a hundred other calves around you, yet you were the only one I saw."

"Stop it," Una whispered back. White Snout couldn't tell by her squint if she was flirting or genuinely dismissive.

"It's true," Titus continued. "I knew right away we belonged together. I felt it in my chest."

"Why do you keep forgetting that I know your tricks by now? Spare me the poetry. I haven't heard you utter such benign things since I was the only one in your harem. These days, your words flow for any youngling your loins take a liking to."

"You know that's not true."

"Do I?" she snapped, momentarily forgetting to whisper. Manius's neck popped upright, his head instinctively scanning the perimeter through half-closed eyelids before drooping back into Quinta's embrace. So, Una wasn't flirting. "Surely it is Nona who has trapped your heart and muddled your mind. Be honest, don't you save your happiness for the young one? She's put you under a spell worse than your heat for Sexta, and even she didn't hold your attention this long. Not that it matters; you'll grow bored as soon as she loses that new scent. It'll be merely another year before you swoon after some other calf, as usual. We're nothing more than feathers in your plumage."

"Una, you know there's more to my decisions than mere whim. It's the way of all kings before me to have outstanding offspring. It's not by the traditions I've created, but by the nature of—"

The wind suddenly shifted, blowing in the opposite direction, and the rest of Titus's words were carried away. Still, White Snout inferred from Una's flat expression that he was reciting a tired litany she'd heard many times before. Una said something in return, but it too was lost to the breeze. When the wind finally died, they both seemed to remember how quiet the night was and lowered their voices further. White Snout strained her neck, ears, and legs as much as she physically could to close the gap without sacrificing her cover. Now, she could hear Titus again.

"I know I haven't been who I used to be, but that's going to change, I promise—and I won't betray my word. After I left the forest today, I remembered why I became king, that much is clear to me now. And when I saw how you took command of everyone like you did, I too remembered how much I owe you. You've been there since the beginning, through the good, the bad, and everything in between, and have often displayed strength when I lack it. You're the backbone that keeps me strong and all of us alive. I've made plenty of mistakes but choosing you as my first was the best decision I've ever made."

His charm softened Una. Her face was as cold as stone until now, but even she had a breaking point. Apparently, this was it.

"It's true," she cooed. "I hold to the traditions because that's when I fell in love with you. You were a leader then, the strongest I'd ever seen, and I've kept that version of you in my heart. I always have."

"Thank you," he said. With her guard lowered, he chanced rubbing his snout against her neck. She pretended to resist at first, only to lean back into him. "I will be that again, you'll see. Sometimes, I wonder if I'm still only around because you protect me."

"Well, someone's gotta. Just don't push your luck."

"I always push my luck with you, Maarika."

Maarika? White Snout thought, her ears perking. *Her real name is Maarika?*

The two pressed their foreheads together, and it was eerie how much they resembled each other. The creases around their eyes bore the same weight of years. Even their teeth gleamed equally bright, and their jaws shared the same long, regal shape. They were, without question, the largest elk White Snout had ever seen, respective to their sexes, of course. And they both wore faces of discipline which, with the right phrase, could be instantly dismantled into an expression of love—exactly as they did right now.

Seeing them like this, truly united, made White Snout feel small in a way her stature never could. She realized she didn't know Titus, not to the extent that she pretended to. But Una did, and in this moment, it was undeniable.

Titus stretched toward Una's ear, and if White Snout hadn't seen his lips flutter in the same manner they did when he whispered to her, she might not have known what he said. But because she had, it might as well have been shouted for every animal in Freyacre to hear.

"You are my beloved *throughout time*. Only you. Don't forget that."

White Snout's throat closed, and her breath froze in place.

PART IX:
WHITE LIE

"**N**ona? Hey, Nona?"

White Snout was oblivious to her surroundings. When Titus first leaned into Una and uttered his vow, with the stolen addition of White Snout's promise of eternity, the weight of his emotional infidelity crashed onto her shoulders like a fallen branch. She collapsed right where she stood, curling into a quaking ball, away from Octava's body heat.

Throughout the night, the bitter sting of betrayal replayed in her mind, looping endlessly as she shivered beneath a thin blanket of snow. Every cherished memory with Titus now felt like a thorn, pricking her heart with each unwelcome recollection.

But somewhere between then and dawn, her trembling jaw slowed until it was still, and her vacant stare locked onto an invisible void. It was as though her spirit abandoned her body, leaving only a hollow shell behind. The foundation of her new life, one naively built on faith in Titus, was nothing more than a figment of an ignorant calf's dream, and so embracing the semblance of death felt like a better refuge than acknowledging the agony ravaging her insides. As time passed, numbness and nothingness intertwined, the world blurring into a dissonant clash of sound and color.

"Nona," Titus repeated for the third time.

If not for Octava's nudge, White Snout's trance might not have been broken by words alone. The rest of the herd was listening attentively to the end of Titus' morning speech, but she couldn't bring herself to look at him, afraid the agony might return. Instead, she nodded slightly, doing as little thinking, and therefore feeling, as possible.

"Tonight, you lie with me, Nona. I apologize for the confusion yesterday. You are all dismissed."

The herd began digging into the snow with their hoofs, uncovering whatever food they could find before the final stretch to the idyllic Grove. While the others chattered eagerly, anticipating what lay ahead, Titus shared none of their excitement. His attention lingered on White Snout, her behavior confirming what he already suspected, that something was wrong. Titus approached her, but White Snout remained still, her vacant gaze fixed on the distance. Not even a twig lay between her lips, her emptiness a sharp contrast to the herd's lively energy.

"I wanted to apologize for last night. You must understand… yesterday, in those woods… I wasn't myself. Please, you must understand and not be bitter."

She looked at him instinctively and winced. There he stood in all of his might and magnificence, his eyes soft in the way she had once desperately sought, yet all she felt was the sting of betrayal. He was dead to her, or worse, a complete and utter stranger. So, what did they have left? Their bond was nothing special, and his promises held no truth. As Una had rightfully pointed out, she was just another feather in his plumage, like all the others, which would've been acceptable, or at least less painful, if only he had acted accordingly.

What broke her was realizing she had wholeheartedly believed in a needless lie—that he loved her and only her *throughout time*. She believed he was kind, personable, and gentle, qualities no other bull had ever demonstrated to her. But she was wrong. She'd thought that, in a similar way he once saved her, she had saved him too. He often remarked how her innocence had rekindled the world's splendor in his eyes. Did he lie about that too? Was that just another hollow platitude, something he spewed to Una, Secunda, Tertia, and the rest of his playthings when in a pinch? Was anything he ever said to her real? She didn't know anymore, and now no longer cared. In a single, callous act, he slayed her trust, revealing she had climbed on air where he convinced her there was rock. She had poured everything into him, except all of it was now lost.

It struck her then that he was just another version of Sharp, older but no wiser. Maybe that was why she was no closer to her father than to Great Horn, because it never mattered. Bulls existed to breed, conquer, and protect, not to love, and certainly not to offer lasting refuge.

"White Snout?" Titus said. He leaned forward to bump his forehead against hers, but her senses kicked back in, turning away sharply.

"Let me be," she said.

He stomped defiantly, though the cows and calves didn't notice amidst their chatter and excitement. "What's the meaning of this? You haven't been yourself."

She felt him searching through her, but he couldn't find what no longer existed. Desperation welled within her as she realized she needed to get through this moment, and every one after it, until they reached the Grove. There, she would rejoin her mother, with or without his blessing. She had to persist, which meant saying whatever it took to get through until she could forget this ever happened.

"Just let me be for now," she said, unsure of what else to do.

He huffed, lingering beside her for a moment longer before reluctantly obeying and sulking away.

Well, now left, and eventually later came. After a lengthy run, the stars began to sparkle against the darkening canvas of the sky. White Snout didn't utter a single word to Titus or anyone else throughout the day, even as he slowed his stride to match hers on many occasions. Every attempt to engage her was futile, lost in the void of her thoughts. Nothing, try as he may, could heal what was broken, his sentiments like fish trying to swim up a waterfall. Nevertheless, he persisted, unaware of what occupied her mind but believing falsely that it was within his power to fix.

When they reached another open field, he halted, as was customary, signaling the herd to form their sleep circle. Anxious to ask what was on White Snout's mind, he wasted no time, trotting toward her without even stopping for a bite of brittle grass after their arduous day.

"Let's get away from the others," he commanded, his tone leaving no room for refusal.

The field stretched barren, interrupted only by a stray bush or a solitary tree. He led her behind one of those solitary trees, its three trunks sprouting from a single gnarled stump. The dwindling light of dusk revealed their closeness to the herd, but the encroaching darkness made it feel as if they were horizons apart. Here, his usual formality fell away, irritation seeping into his voice.

"Tell me, what's the meaning behind your behavior? If you have a grievance, spit it out already!"

Even alone with the king, she felt nothing where ecstasy had once bloomed. The gap between them felt insurmountable, and she couldn't bring herself to believe it could be closed. During the day's run, she had tried to justify him, letting the faintest voice in her head rise to his defense. But reason had swiftly beaten it back into silence.

Merely standing before him was a stark reminder of the contrast between them. When his head pressed against Una's, they seemed alike—equals. When White Snout stood before him, her head barely reached his chest, and although that may seem trivial, it exemplified very clearly the years that separated them. Her life was just beginning. How could she love someone who had lived so much without her, seen things she might never understand, and lied so effortlessly to serve himself? Though a giant stood before her, he felt as powerless as a fly in her eyes. Even if she wanted to love him again, her heart had already sealed its decision.

"Titus... it's just... it's just—"

"It's just what?" he egged.

As she began to speak, her throat quivered. Though she projected indifference, perhaps deep down, she wasn't as detached as she wanted to be. Perhaps she was scared. "It's just... I... I don't love you."

She didn't know what to expect but assumed he'd be angry. Still, she wasn't sure how that anger would manifest, even fearing briefly that he might charge at her. But he didn't speak or move, at least not immediately. His breath fell silent, though a cloud of vapor still rose steadily from his nostrils into the chilled air.

"Do you feel as though I cannot protect you? I recognize I've made my share of mistakes, but I assure you, those are in the past."

"It's not that," she said, choosing her words carefully. She refrained from disclosing the real reason behind her decision, sparing herself from reliving her darkest moment. She couldn't bear to return to that night, trembling beneath a blanket of snow, her heart shattered into as many pieces as there were stars in the sky.

Luckily, he didn't press her further. Instead, he carried on entirely on his own, his attitude shifting to shallow confidence, as if her words weren't absolute. "Oh, I see. You're upset because I lay with Una last night. If I'd known you'd react this way, I wouldn't have let it happen. But you must understand, what I witnessed in those woods, what the wolves did, I wasn't myself.

Show some compassion and be reasonable. I know you still love me. You're just afraid."

"I'm not," she sighed, growing weary. "I just want to go home."

He hummed in relief, his breathing steadying back to normal. "Of course, you miss your mother! You behave so maturely that I almost forget how young you are. This is natural, but you'll see her again soon. And if you go with her, it's only a matter of time before you'll miss me too. Trust me."

Trust me. The words echoed off the walls of her skull, igniting a dormant spark that erupted into a raging inferno. She longed to headbutt his knee, or kick his jaw with her hind leg, or curse his name to Freyacre, begging the spirit to sweep him away with a powerful gust of wind. Each utterance from his deceitful lips felt like a poisonberry spreading across her tongue.

How could she have ever loved such a loathsome creature? The warning signs had been glaringly obvious, embodied by the eight examples trailing him daily, and now she was the ninth. She had been blind to those signs before, but now they were all she could see.

His last words triggered a shift within her. She too puffed out her chest and rooted her legs firmly into the ground. The trembling in her throat vanished, replaced by a defiance that rang declared itself unmistakably in her tone.

"No, *trust me*, Titus, I'm leaving. Once we reach the Grove, I'm going back with my—"

"To hell with the Grove," he snapped, feeding off her tenacity and matching thunder with thunder. "We'll get there, but tonight is our only night alone until then. Ever since I saw how cruel the wolves can really be, I've sought nothing but your soothing touch. You're so delicate, and so beautiful, and small—you remind me why I wanted to be king in the first place; to protect elk like you. Even your white snout, I've never seen anything so beautiful in all my life. It's simply—"

He rambled, recounting fragments of their shared history, sprinkling in his own, and even divulging random fantasies about her, and then some. But his compliments, stories, and lies only stoked the flames of her wrath. Nothing he confessed was special, his generic performance only reinforcing its worthlessness. When he finished, he chuckled at some bad joke he made, but when her lips remained flat, his voice faded into silence.

"You can no longer change my mind. I'm going home," she declared again.

He looked lost. They were having two separate conversations, neither listening to the other, yet both unwavering in their stance. Titus didn't even understand why she was angry, and White Snout didn't care that he didn't. In this game of push-and-pull, as she backed away, he was going all in. Their stares locked in a silent battle of wills until he broke away, circling her slowly while she stood motionless, facing forward.

"Fine. If you insist, you may rejoin your mother," he said at last. Her fur bristled, for she knew better. This was no concession, just another ruse to win her back. She was learning his tactics. "As much as I treasure our bond, I won't hold you back. I'm no predator, just an elk in love. But until then, allow me to try to win your heart back properly while I still can—a fool's hope it may be."

Suddenly, his chest brushed her hind legs, and his breath heated the nape of her neck. What fleeting confidence she had vanished instantly, leaving her trembling like when she was blanketed in the snow alone. She wanted to run, sensing what was coming. But where could she run? She didn't know the location of the Grove, where her mother awaited, and even if she did, there was no outrunning Titus. The wolves, too, might be lurking, ready to pounce on any that might stray. For now, she had no choice but to remain with the herd she loathed.

He stretched his neck forward, his lips near her ears while his body remained behind. "You do love me, White Snout. You'll soon remember."

She felt his waist buckle as he shifted his weight toward his hips as his front legs pressed against her shoulders. Her vision blurred, stomach churned, and her legs jittered harder than they ever had. She realized with chilling clarity that she was helpless, just as helpless as when she saw a wolf attacking her mother. There was nothing she could do to prevent what was imminent.

—Or maybe there was.

She *had* acted when a wolf clung to her mother's side. She had charged forward, spurred on by nothing but hope, no matter how futile it seemed. She had been fully aware she was quite possibly running to her death but believed wholeheartedly it was better to die trying to save her mother than die idle. Now, she needed to summon that courage again, but this time, to save herself.

Her body acted on its own, shrugging him off with a hard grunt and turning to face him, her frame tensed. And there he was, the king, standing just as steadfast as her with his eyes narrowing into a squint. Although she made the decision, the act of defiance still felt surreal, as though it belonged to someone else. Her throat tightened, but she fought through it.

"Titus, I'm not yours anymore," she said firmly.

He stepped closer, his broad chest filling her vision while his head loomed high above.

"Do you know what tradition commands when you defy a king?" he asked.

She swallowed hard as countless images flashed through her mind—none in her favor.

"I doubt you want to find out," he murmured so lowly, it could be mistaken for a whisper of wind.

Judging by the heat of his breath, she felt his head creep closer until his lips brushed against her ear. Though her stance did not falter, she remained frozen in place not knowing what else to do. Her mind raced for a solution, and just as he leaned to nibble her ear again, an idea sprang to mind, foolish perhaps, but better than nothing.

"It's your teeth," she blurted. "That's why I'm upset. I don't like your teeth."

His warm breath paused. Perplexed, he stepped back. "My teeth?"

She pressed on. "Yes, they're too sharp. The sharpest I've ever seen on an elk."

"Of course they're the sharpest," he declared proudly. "I could crush bone with the power of my jaw."

"I know, but they hurt me." She feigned a pout, playing into his delight in her perceived fragility. "Every time we're alone, you hurt me. You said it yourself, I'm delicate, but you treat me like you're dueling a bull. Have you forgotten romance?"

The deception felt unnatural on her tongue, but for survival, she would wear any hide. He had already proven he'd do the same, so she was merely returning lie for lie. Still, she was surprised by the effectiveness. By targeting his physicality, she saw him flinch. For all his strength, his ego was left unguarded, a weakness she hadn't expected. She attacked further.

"And you're always eating. Every time we graze, you eat more than all the first years combined, and they're growing!"

"Of course I do! I'm bigger than all five of them combined!" he protested.

"But don't you think you're getting too big—at least for someone as small as me? Or do you eat more because you're getting older? How old are you, anyway? I've always wondered."

His squint faded, and his big eyes returned wide with hesitation. She had struck him successfully again.

"It doesn't matter. I'm the strongest I've ever been, and I eat as much as I can to stay strong. And my teeth are sharp to grind the food that makes me strong. I can beat anyone."

Unconsciously, White Snout strode forward as he continued to withdraw.

"If you want me to love you like I used to, I need to desire you again."

Even in the darkness, she noticed his shoulders droop. She had one week left until she would be reunited with her mother, and if lying is what it took to protect herself, she'd do it. She only had one priority, like Una said—survival.

As Titus retreated further from the moonlight into the shadow of the three-forked tree, she tried her luck at walking away, and this time, he didn't bother stopping her.

PART X:
NARROW RETURN

When the morning sun bathed White Snout in its warmth and loosened her eyelids with its light, she almost believed she was back beside her mother. She yawned deeply, stretching her legs as far as they would go, before a shiver caused her to curl back into a ball. She would've drifted back to sleep if not for the shrill, high-pitched noises from the eight other cows nearby, standing in a tight circle. Only then did White Snout realize she hadn't been forced awake at dawn by a hoof prodding her ribs.

"I don't know what's gotten into him. His eyes are bloodshot. Must've been up all night," Secunda said.

Una shook her head. "Whatever it is, the calves think it's some kind of game. As old as I am, Titus still manages to surprise me with just how stupid he can be."

"Perhaps it's part of their leadership training," Tertia suggested.

"Not that I've ever seen," Una replied. The others exchanged questioning glances, but no one ventured an explanation.

White Snout turned to the five first-year bulls just beyond the circle of mothers, their bellies shaking with laughter, a first since she'd joined them.

"I got the largest one," Brutus proclaimed proudly, sucking on a pebble so big that half of it jutted out from between his lips.

"Nu-uh," Jovian said, his voice garbled by the rock in his mouth. "I'm *woing.*"

Gallus, Otho, and Manius also had rocks of various sizes in their mouths, each grunting incomprehensibly as they argued whose was the biggest. White Snout didn't know what to draw from their strange behavior until Titus appeared at the far side of the field. The cows' gossip was confirmed.

Were it not for his distinctive size, White Snout might have mistaken him for another elk entirely. His gait was slow and meandering, reminiscent of those nearing Great Horn's age. As he plodded closer, she noticed his eyes were indeed bloodshot with heavy bags sagging beneath them, and his chest rose and fell with labored breaths. His cheeks bulged unnaturally, and when he halted an appropriate distance away, he spat out a stone that dwarfed those of the calves, though it hadn't protruded from his lips.

"Line up," he ordered, his voice weak and devoid of its usual authority.

Though the cows had spoken boldly in their circle before, none were brave enough to voice their concerns in the presence of their leader. Silently, they lined up as commanded. The first-year bulls followed, also spitting out their rocks with varying reluctance. Once the herd had assembled, Titus nodded toward a distant mountain range, its many crests barely visible against the rising sun. However, White Snout couldn't focus on where he gestured. Her attention fixed on his foam-flecked muzzle, where drool dripped onto the scattered stones below. The eerie dawn cast a ruddy glow across the ground, making the saliva-coated surfaces gleam with an unsettling sheen.

"The Grove is on the other side of that range. Since you had extra time this morning, I trust you all ate plenty. We don't stop until the sun is at its peak."

He dismissed them with a quick snort, sucked the stone back into his mouth, and began trotting in the direction of the Grove. The others, including White Snout, stood frozen, stunned by his abruptness and the strange scene they'd just witnessed.

Normally, his speeches were long, often cutting into the allotted time for grazing. But today, he provided no clarity for his strange behavior, no motivational words, and not even a cheerful mention of their proximity to their promised destination—the end of their quest. He didn't explain anything to anyone, leaving everyone questioning, except for White Snout.

As they ran that day, she didn't have to wonder why he ground a rock against teeth. By the afternoon break, she understood why he only sipped water while the others grazed. And as night fell, she knew why he was utterly exhausted, unlike the harem, who relied on hushed guesses.

"I just don't understand. Is he fasting for a feast at the Grove? I know it's said to have greens year-round, but why starve yourself?" Sexta said. "Now my little Jovian says he won't eat. He claims he's being just as disciplined as the king."

"Titus loves being the center of attention," Septima said. "Why would this be any different? He wants to show off his appetite in front of the herds."

Una turned about to ensure the young bulls weren't with earshot but paid no mind to White Snout, who was nearby. "Even so, that doesn't explain the rock in his mouth."

Sexta shifted her weight uneasily from one hoof to the other, while Septima's ears flicked in confusion.

When the second day arrived, Titus seemed more energetic, running at his usual pace and temporarily silencing the cows' chatter. But on the third day, his vigor waned, and he moved slower than ever, slow enough for White Snout to keep pace. By the fourth day, he still had consumed nothing but water, and his frame looked leaner, the robust curve of his sides beginning to hollow beneath his winter coat.

Until then, everyone had refrained from speaking to Titus directly about his strange behavior and its influence on the first-year bulls, who eagerly mimicked him in youthful competition. But on the fifth morning, after yet another short and uninspired speech, Una's concern finally overcame her.

"Titus," she said, addressing him in front of the herd.

He had turned up the slope, determined to finish ascending the mountain that day and begin their descent toward the Grove the next. When Una called after him, however, he paused and looked back, his neck drooping under the weight of his great antlers.

"What is the meaning of this?" she pressed. "Are you training the bulls? Preparing for a feast? We are your harem. We have the right to know."

Titus surveyed the herd, exhaustion etched into every line of his face. His gaze lingered on White Snout for a moment before his expression hardened.

"Who says you have the *right* to know?" His voice was raspy, his words more jumbled than clear.

For once, Una's jaw quivered. After a brief hesitation, she said in a near whisper, "me."

Titus turned fully toward her, closing the gap until their chests nearly touched, their breaths forming a shared cloud in the frigid air. He lifted his head to its full height, rising above the cows like the mountain and casting a long shadow across the ground.

"Is that so?" His half-closed eyes widened with sudden intensity, dominating his face. "Have you forgotten I AM YOUR KING? Your rights are WHAT I SAY THEY ARE!"

His voice echoed across the mountainside, shaking the earth beneath their hooves. Without another word, he turned and trudged onward, leaving the herd to follow with trembling legs up the remainder of the slope.

Titus' behavior teetered on the edge of an outburst as they ascended the mountain. The slightest inconvenience set him off. He stomped his hooves and grumbled like a calf whenever he slipped on ice or stumbled over loose ground. If a cow or calf came too close or accidentally brushed against him, he lowered his head menacingly and let out a warning snort, startling everyone and heightening the tension. At times, he halted in his tracks, blocking the path for anyone behind him and forcing a pause in their climb. And so, no one, not even Una, dared risk upsetting him further.

He maintained the rock in his mouth, ate nothing at each rest, and grew weaker as the sun crossed the sky. Despite his deteriorating state, the first-year bulls persisted in their strange routines, still convinced they were playing games to prove their superiority to the eleven herds awaiting them at the Grove. Yet even they began to falter, their energy and resolve waning under the grueling ascent.

Through it all, White Snout clung to the joy of being so close to her mother. Her heart leapt at the thought of returning to her loving embrace and reuniting with her calfhood herd and half-siblings. The thought of belonging, of feeling at home, spurred her forward with eager determination. So much so, She had to temper her pace to avoid outstripping the bulls, whose steps slowed more with each passing hour.

The mountain, large and snow-covered, seemed a small obstacle if it meant her mother waited on the other side. This thought kept her warm against the frigid wind, urged her to take another step even when her legs burned, and made her feel alive amidst the wintry landscape. By the time they reached the crest that night, she couldn't bear to wait until morning to begin their descent. She longed to forgo sleep, to dash down the opposite slope as fast as her legs could carry her, and tumble into her mother's embrace in the sanctuary of the Grove.

The other cows, puzzled and moody from their king's strange behavior, were heartened by the spirited determination of their youngest member. Her energy was infectious, lifting their spirits and making them merrier as their anticipation grew. They, too, longed for the verdant embrace of the Grove, hungry for the bounty it promised and curious about its mysteries.

For them, it was more than a destination, it was a myth come to life, a story passed through generations of a sacred haven with enough greens to sustain every elk in Freyacre. From their conversations, White Snout gathered that it was once the basin of an ancient lake, surrounded by skyward cliffs and accessible only by a tunnel. According to legend, the original twelve elk leaders had collapsed the tunnel long ago to protect it, sealing it away until the day it might be needed. Though grim necessity had driven them to seek refuge there, the prospect of rediscovering a place said to bring peace filled them with hope and excitement.

Running day after day was something they could endure, sure, but it was far from enjoyable. Yes, they trained ruthlessly and upheld archaic traditions, but they also daydreamed of well-deserved rest, free from the threat of lurking wolves or the duty of alerting another herd. Each cow clung to a hope that helped them bury their unease about their king, imagining his fasting served a grand purpose beyond their understanding. The mystery of his behavior stirred curiosity and excitement among the herd—all except for White Snout, who knew the truth. It made sleep for everyone nearly impossible that night. White Snout stirred awake often just to stare out at the stars as her thoughts drifted to the one being that brought her solace.

I can't wait to see you, she thought, longing for her mother's presence.

"I can't believe we're almost there! Just imagine, real food at last!" Quinta exclaimed as they descended the mountain the next day.

"Not just food! I heard the Grove has fireweed taller than me!" Quarta gushed, leaping over a boulder in excitement, something she'd never dare if stamina mattered. "Can you imagine? We could feast for days!"

"Do you think it even has globemallows? My mother used to tell me how sweet they are. What if they're as delicious as she claimed?"

Quarta's excitement bubbled over. "What if they're even better? I bet we'll have to fend off the first years just to get a bite!"

Quinta flicked her lips in mock defiance. "Oh, I'd like to see them try! I'd push Manius out of the way to get a head start."

The two erupted in laughter.

This shared enthusiasm, combined with the relief of having scaled the mountain the day before, made the descent feel easy—practically a leisurely stroll for the cows. Though it took the entire day to reach the bottom, by nightfall White Snout and the others were brimming with energy, evident in their restless legs and upright postures. They weren't breathing heavy clouds into the air like the worn bulls who trailed a great distance behind. Instead, they chatted excitedly, their thrill manifesting into loud, eager calls that echoed through the crisp night air.

"Where do you think the tunnel is?" Sexta said, scanning the base of the mountainside with wide, hopeful eyes. "I bet it's so well hidden, it's right in front of our faces!"

Quinta chuckled. "It could be! Maybe it's hidden under vines or covered in moss. Wouldn't that be a clever trick?"

Sexta nodded eagerly, her tail flicking with anticipation. "Or maybe it's behind a waterfall! I've heard stories of caves that only appear under the right light."

"Now that's just absurd. Exhaustion had stolen your senses," Secunda chimed in, before bursting into a hearty laugh.

Even Una, who had been quietly observing, seemed to feed off their energy, her stern facade softening in the warmth of their giddy fervor. "It's close. I can feel it."

"You really think so, Una?" Sexta asked, her voice laced with excitement. "What if we stumble upon it any moment now? Just imagine!"

"Just imagine!" Quinta echoed, her breath catching at the thought. "A secret place where we can finally rest, free from the wolves. It feels like a dream!"

"It's more than a dream," Una replied, her tone still serious yet tinged with hope. "It's a chance for us to reclaim our peace."

Sexta's gaze grew contemplative. "If it's as special as they say, it might be the start of something new for all of us. We could tell our own stories to new calves and become part of the legend they'll carry on."

"Yeah..." Septima added, her excitement suddenly fading, her voice trailing off in a way that invited a hush. She rarely spoke to anyone besides Sexta and Octava, so her words carried an unexpected weight. "I just want everyone to know, I couldn't have made it without you. You're all like family to me. Both my parents are gone, and I've only birthed females... so this is precious to me."

The others fell silent, exchanging glances and nodding in agreement. As far as White Snout knew, none of them had ever expressed affection for one another, except the mothers toward their sons. This was likely the closest they had ever come to calling one another family. The excitement in the air lingered but was now laced with an unexpected sense of bonding. Admittedly, White Snout felt closer to them too—still estranged, but closer than ever before, which wasn't saying much.

Having reached the base of the mountain first, the cows allowed themselves this rare moment of reprieve. Their shared joy hung in the air, fragile but genuine, until Titus barreled into the center of their gathering, shattering the brief respite. The first-year bulls followed, visibly exhausted and panting, their sides heaving with tremendous effort.

Once gathered, the cows hurriedly lined up, their anxiety palpable as they awaited their king's direction. But Titus didn't address them. Instead, he staggered to a nearby boulder and collapsed against it. It was clear he was weak, his legs trembling as he struggled to stay upright after the grueling trek. He seemed utterly indifferent to everything else, consumed entirely by the overwhelming need to rest.

The herd waited patiently, their silence heavy with tension. Despite their king's feeble state, they understood even a sliver of his remaining strength could still overpower them if he chose to assert it. What's more, they knew he was just one good meal away from regaining his full power, and no one wanted to face the wrath of his renewed rage. So close to the feast, so near the promise of the Grove, they convinced themselves his erratic behavior would soon end.

Eventually, he stood, and when he noticed their tense frames, his expression shifted to one of annoyance and confusion.

"Well, what are you all waiting for? Make a sleep circle," he said.

He turned away, dismissing them as the cows exchanged uncertain glances, some nervous, others angry. He was breaking his promise, or at least the hope he had kindled in them.

Una, ever reliable, took charge. "But—" Suddenly, her throat tightened, her courage faltering after yesterday's public reprimand, leaving her words unfinished.

To everyone's surprise, Titus turned back to her, an unsettling glint in his eyes, somewhere between amusement and menace. "I know what you're going to ask; where's the Grove?"

The cows and first-year bulls stayed silent as he heaved himself off the boulder, his heavy steps crunching through the snow as he drew closer.

"It's close," he continued. "Truthfully, my memory has grown hazy with time. But in the morning, when the light reveals the way, rest assured, we'll be there—I promise you all. In the meantime, let's get some rest. Tomorrow will be quite packed with celebration. Remember, we are Freyacre's chosen."

His voice was gentle, too tired to carry anger, yet an unsettling undercurrent lingered, enough to make White Snout shiver. Despite her unease, the promise seemed to appease the cows and calves. They broke into a blissful dance, skipping in a circle as though fear had never existed. Even Una looked young again, her eyes shedding their apprehension in a rare moment of sheer joy as she watched her son leap into the air alongside his half-brothers. Weak as he was, Titus managed to summon enough energy to skip alongside his calves and cows.

After the dance ended and a few more laughs and tales were shared, the herd settled into a warm huddle, the night air still biting despite their restless bodies. To White Snout's surprise, Una caught her eye and nodded toward an empty space beside her, inviting her closer.

"Come here, young one. You earned it."

A flicker of resentment flared within White Snout, kindled by memories of Una's constant judgment and derision. Una had made her life miserable at every turn, relishing any opportunity to undermine her place in the herd. For reasons White Snout could scarcely comprehend, perhaps rooted in Una's insecurities or past grievances, the elder cow often acted as though White Snout's very existence was a personal affront. Yet, with the cold creeping in and the promise of her mother and a feast just one sunrise away, she considered setting their feud aside, even if only for the night. Reluctantly, White Snout stepped beside her, folding her legs and seeking comfort in the shared body heat, grateful for the warmth from the other cows surrounding her as well. She tried to push aside her hatred for Una as she settled into a moment of peace. But the camaraderie didn't last.

Just as White Snout's muscles relaxed, Titus approached the huddle, his intense expression shattering her brief respite and making it clear he wanted something.

"Nona?" he said.

White Snout nearly forgot her formal title until she felt the weight of the other cows' eyes on her.

"Come with me," he said.

The cheerful hum of conversation among the cows fell into an awkward silence. Sexta, whose turn it was to spend the night with the king, seemed on the verge of speaking but ultimately refrained, her unease quickly shifting to relief, likely grateful to be excused.

"Come now," Titus repeated, his tone sharper as he trotted toward a veil of twisted, dark trees at the base of the slope. The trees formed a jagged circle around the incline, expanding into a shadowy forest that disappeared behind the mountain's curve. It offered them seclusion, away from the herd.

White Snout stayed rooted in place, every fiber of her being resisting his command. She loathed the idea of being alone with him, her legs trembling with suppressed defiance. For a fleeting moment, she considered bugling as loudly as she could, hoping against hope her mother might hear her distress. But then Una nudged her gently, a silent encouragement cutting through her hesitation. White Snout's heart sank as she realized she had no other choice. Refusal wasn't an option—not with Titus, nor with the herd's collective gaze pressing down on her like a suffocating force.

She exhaled slowly, her heart heavy with dread. Only one night separated her from her mother—just one night. She reminded herself she could endure this, no matter how difficult it might be. She had survived everything else so far.

Her legs felt impossibly heavy as she plodded toward the tree line. Passing through the ethereal boundary where moonlight surrendered to the darkness, she noticed a massive shadow sprawled across the earth. A faint beam of light slipped through a sliver in the tree canopy, illuminating Titus' large, round eyes

"I've taken your desires to heart. Now, come to me," he said, his voice strained with a mixture of weariness and something deeper. When she didn't move closer, he tilted his head, confused by her hesitation. "Please, give me this night with you. I have done as you asked. All this, I have done to show my devotion to you."

His words fell impotently against her stone exterior, unable to reach the core of her being. White Snout felt nothing—no sympathy, no sorrow. Her mind was too consumed by the thought of tomorrow, too preoccupied with the joy of reuniting with her mother. The present held no power over her. If anything, she felt embarrassed for him. The once-great king, now reduced to a heap on the ground, begged for affection like a calf seeking approval.

Perhaps, in his own twisted way, he did love her. Or maybe it wasn't love at all, but something more selfish. He loved himself so much that the very idea of rejection was intolerable. It wasn't devotion that drove him, but desperation, a frantic need to preserve his unchallenged world and keep his pride intact.

She stood there, watching him, unmoved by his actions or the pitiful sight before her. Her heart, once bound to the king, now resided elsewhere, far beyond the trees, beyond the cold night, waiting for the promise of a new dawn.

"Titus, I told you, I'm rejoining my calfhood herd," she said firmly. "I no longer wish to be part of your harem."

With a heavy huff, he mustered the strength to stand, his massive figure looming over her. Even in his feeble state, he radiated a raw, intimidating power. A single flex of his muscles could easily subdue her if his mood darkened, regardless of the pathetic expression etched across his worn face.

"Please," he said, his voice barely above a whisper. "Let me try to win you back."

She remained silent as he leaned down to nibble at her ear... and his teeth were shockingly soft. He moved toward her hind legs, and when his body buckled against hers, she felt how much lighter he had become—almost weightless compared to before. Yet, even with this radical transformation, she felt no desire for him. Rather, she found herself more repelled than she thought possible. His touch, once commanding and thrilling, had become insistent and unwelcome.

As his head brushed against her, one of his antlers pricked her skin, and she shrugged him off.

"What is it now?" he groaned.

She turned to face him, and for a fleeting moment, she wondered if she was the cruel one. Had her words cut him too deeply? She hadn't intended to wound him so profoundly or let their private conflict ripple through the herd, but deep down, she knew there was no turning back. She had to leave this behind. She didn't care for him, not this broken version, not the powerful king he once was, nor any form that might follow. Her heart had emptied itself of love long ago, and nothing he could do or say would ever restore it. Once, he had everything; her mind, body, and spirit. Now, he had nothing. In fact, less than nothing, for she realized she would show more empathy to a stranger than she could muster for him now.

"It's, uh, your antlers. They hurt me," she said, the lie so thin it wouldn't have fooled even herself. She began to trot away, hoping his brittle pride would defeat him, but the sound of his hoof stomping the ground froze her in place.

"My antlers?" he said, his voice wavering, uneven. "Oh, just my antlers? As if they won't fall off when the time comes. But no, the problem is *now*—my antlers."

She glanced back, her heart sinking. She had seen many sides of Titus; the tough Titus, the strong Titus, the indifferent Titus, and the disciplining Titus, but this one felt disturbingly familiar. It reminded her of the version who had emerged from the forbidden forest, where the Boundary lay hidden, the place no elk dared to cross. The Titus who had returned from there had thrashed his head wildly, consumed by something otherworldly, and this felt no different.

"My teeth, my weight, and now my antlers too? Of course, my antlers are to blame. Would it be my skin next? Should I rid myself of that as well?" His voice started calm but grew darker and more unhinged with each repetition. "My antlers! MY antlers. It's only *my* antlers. *Of course*, they're the problem!"

She shriveled in place, her back hoof stiffening and her fur bristling as the urge to flee surged within her. But, like before, she knew there was nowhere to run. Even if she bolted, he would chase her down with ease.

"Y-yes, your antlers. We'll wait for them to fall off. T-then we can be together again, Titus," she bluffed desperately. She only needed one more night, just one more, to reach her mother, her sanctuary. "Maybe—"

Her words faltered and died as his glare bore into her, stifling her breath. His eyes, unnervingly wide, seemed to glow as though lit from within.

"I am king! I do not wait!" he seethed, his voice quivering with fury.

Without warning, he stormed over to a nearby tree with two trunks sprouting from the same base. He wedged his right antler between the trunks and twisted his neck violently, once, then twice, then three times, the force of each movement making the heavy branches sway wildly above them.

"Stop it! I didn't mean it!" she cried, water welling in her eyes. Her stomach churned, disgusted that a desperate lie had spiraled into such grave and unintended consequences. All she wanted was to return to her mother, to the simple peace of her calfhood herd. She had never asked for any of this; the influence, the attention, or the suffocating burden of his obsession. She had been happy, content in her former life, but Titus refused to listen. He refused to let her go.

On the fourth twist, a loud snap echoed through the night, and his massive antler fell cleanly from its root. Blood bubbled at the side of his head, a red trail trickling past his eye and staining his fur. Creeping toward her, his jaw slack and saliva glistening on his lips, he no longer resembled the majestic king she once knew.

She felt trapped in a surreal nightmare, her eyes fixed on the fallen antler—a grotesque image of love and sacrifice. Amid this perverse display, a lone owl hooted, its mournful cry lamenting the distortion of nature it bore witness to.

"Compromise, you see?" Titus rasped, his voice growing manic. "One antler for you and one for me. We'll tell the others we were caught off guard in the forest by a dozen predators, and I valiantly defended you. They'll love it! Now, accept me!"

She tried to speak, but he paid her no mind. Summoning his might, he overpowered her, rising on his hind legs as she crumpled underneath him. Her lies had worked until now, but there was never a chance she could win against brute strength. She felt him fumbling behind her, and just as he was about to take charge, she closed her eyes, meaningless noise spilling from her throat. Terror gripped her entirely, and in a final, desperate plea, she prayed to Freyacre and the stars that this nightmare would soon pass.

Get me through this, momma, her thoughts cried.

Then suddenly, there was a noise, heavy, swift hooves pounding the earth, snapping both her and Titus' attention back to the world around them. He leapt off White Snout just as Una broke through the tree line, her face etched with apprehension so deep that Titus' missing antler escaped her notice.

"Come with me," Una said, her voice tight with urgency.

"What is it?" Titus snapped, his eyes narrowing.

If Una's speed hadn't made the urgency clear, her tone certainly did. "Don't delay! It's Carnos."

Titus didn't spare White Snout a second glance. Straightening to his full height, he darted out from under the forest canopy with astonishing speed, his weakened state a mystery if one didn't know better.

White Snout nearly followed, ready to storm after him and Una to defend her herd, just as her mother would have. But as she was about to take a step forward, she hesitated, the weight of everything she had endured holding her back. After another second of consideration, she chose to stay right where she was... shrouded in the darkness of the forest that hugged the base of the mountain.

Even from her concealed position, she spotted the giant wolf, Carnos, leading his seemingly endless pack, their amber eyes glowing like lightning in the dark. She watched as Titus made his grand entrance, positioning himself at the head of the triangle formation with the eight cows divided evenly on either side. Carnos nodded toward Titus' crown of antlers, noticing the missing half, and smirked. Enraged, Titus charged, but when he positioned his remaining antler under Carnos' belly, he couldn't lift him—not anymore. The strength that had once defined the elk king was gone, leaving him vulnerable.

The five first-year bulls, Brutus, Manius, Otho, Jovian, and Gallus, charged forward from behind their mothers. In their youthful inexperience, they attacked wildly, biting at Carnos' ankles instead of using the headbutts or kicks instinctive to adult elk. Their efforts, driven by desperate energy, were clumsy and uncoordinated.

Carnos merely threw his head back and howled with laughter at the night sky, "their teeth, it tickles!"

At that moment, Titus turned his head, glancing in White Snout's direction. For a fleeting second, she believed their eyes met, a connection that stole her breath. Then, with brutal swiftness, Carnos leapt onto Titus' back, forcing the weakened king to collapse under his weight.

Wolves began pouring down the mountainside like an avalanche, their howls echoing with the thrill of impending victory. Soon, White Snout lost sight of Titus, the cows, and the young bulls altogether as the battlefield dissolved into a chaotic landscape of gray fur. The air was pierced by a chilling symphony of sounds; the gleeful howls of wolves, competitive snarls fighting over the best meat, and the mournful wails of elk caught in nature's unforgiving grasp. The savage reality unfolded before her, carving itself into her memory as a haunting vision destined to invade her dreams forever.

She had never intended for any of this to unfold, but the urgency to flee now outweighed all the other impulses. The wolves were close, and if they caught her scent, she'd be next. With no refuge in sight, and no mother or king to shield her from danger, the crushing weight of solitude pressed upon her, leaving her utterly vulnerable in the unforgiving wilderness.

Her gaze lingered on the spot where Titus had last stood, now swallowed by the ravenous pack. Whispering, or perhaps only thinking, she murmured sorrowfully, "goodbye, my beloved." She willed herself to run, but fear rooted her in place, her body refusing to obey.

Freyacre, give me my mother's strength, she prayed. Then, as if answering her plea, her legs suddenly loosened. Trembling but moving, they carried her away from the wolves and deeper into the tangled forest. Her heart thundered in her ears, a frantic rhythm of fear and determination. The wolves' howls echoed through the trees, chasing her like shadows. But she didn't look back. She couldn't. Instead, she pushed herself forward faster and faster, desperate to put as much distance as she could between herself and the nightmare unraveling behind her.

Once a sanctuary, the trees presently seemed to conspire against her. Every branch and thorn reached out to snag her fur, every root threatened to trip her. The relentless howls of the wolves clawed at her ears, spurring her onward in a desperate, mindless dash for survival. She had no sense of time, whether only moments had passed or an eternity. The world blurred around her, her instincts fraying under the weight of exhaustion and terror.

All the training from her youth, lessons in endurance, escape, and the endless games of hide-and-chase, felt utterly useless now. Delirium clouded her mind, and her legs faltered beneath her. She stumbled over a log, crashed hard into a tree trunk, and collapsed on the frozen ground, the impact rattling through her bones. Dizzy and disoriented, she blinked, struggling to clear her vision, but the fog of exhaustion refused to lift.

Through the haze, she glanced up, her gaze unfocused. She found herself at the edge of the forest, the skyward mountain looming overhead, its summit crowned by a brilliant full moon. She thought she saw the faint outline of a cave at the mountain's base as two shadowy figures approached, growing larger with every step. She couldn't discern whether they brought salvation or danger, but her body had no strength left to flee.

Summoning the last of her will, she whispered a soft, fragile promise, her voice barely a breath as the dark silhouettes closed in. "I'm coming home, momma."

And then, whether it was a dream or reality, a warm voice filled her ears, comforting and familiar.

"You *are* home, White Snout."

At last, winter's tight grip released. Twigs began budding, and green slowly crept where there once was snow. Spring gently roused Freyacre from dreams woven from memories of the past and visions of what might come, beneath the eye of the old sun. Fire, water, and wind carved fresh faces into its body, just as they had always done, while life continued to ebb and flow. So Freyacre did not fret a distant dawn, when man would one day give it shape.

The great spirit stretched, shaking the snow from its crown, and gave the eagle new heights to build its nest. As it yawned, the rivers stirred in its veins, coursing with renewed vigor. The bear emerged from its cave, eager to fill its stomach with fresh fish, and the beaver, ever industrious, reshaped the flowing waters with its dam.

Freyacre pushed new green shoots from its womb, offering the rabbit tender grasses and clover. The snake, slithering out from its winter burrow, explored the lush thickets of the spirit's skin. Meanwhile, the squirrel left the shelter of its hollow tree and scurried along one of Freyacre's many fingers, searching for fresh buds and seeds hidden in the canopy.

Freyacre played no favorites, for its nature was impartial, yet it had always watched over certain creatures a bit more closely. One of these was the elk calf Titus, born a giant and destined for great purpose. As the spirit spread its gifts across the land, it searched high and low for the one who had become the mighty king of the elk. But despite all of Freyacre's eyes and its far-reaching presence, it could not find him. The mighty king of the elk, his harem, and the paths he forged, vanished like mist at dawn.

Though to its delight, Freyacre found White Snout, hidden away in a place long abandoned. She had changed, most notably in the way her belly had begun to swell. Titus had sired an heir, and it pleased the spirit, knowing that the elk herds would be led not by the antlers of a proud king, but by the cunning direction of a white snout.

www.ingramcontent.com/pod-product-compliance
Lightning Source LLC
Chambersburg PA
CBHW010133150626
46552CB00024B/3254